Human V

Penelope Fitzgerald h
children, an economist, a Spanish
phsiologist. The family used to live on Thame
barge, which sank, but are now settled in
London and in Somerset. *Human Voices* is her
fourth novel. *Offshore* won, and *The Bookshop*
was shortlisted for, the Booker Prize. Her
seventh novel, *Nellie and Lisa*, was published
by Collins in 1988.

also by Penelope Fitzgerald

Penelope Fitzgerald

HUMAN VOICES

FLAMINGO
Published by Fontana Paperbacks

First published by William Collins Sons and Co. Ltd., 1980

This Flamingo edition published in 1988 by
Fontana Paperbacks, 8 Grafton Street, London W1X 3LA

Typeset in Linotron Baskerville
Printed and bound in Great Britain by
William Collins Sons and Co.Ltd., Glasgow

1

Inside Broadcasting House, the Department of Recorded Programmes was sometimes called the Seraglio, because its Director found that he could work better when surrounded by young women. This in itself was an understandable habit and quite harmless, or, to be more accurate, RPD never considered whether it was harmless or not. If he was to think about such things, his attention had to be specially drawn to them. Meanwhile it was understood by the girls that he might have an overwhelming need to confide his troubles in one of them, or perhaps all of them, but never in two of them at once, during the three wartime shifts in every twenty-four hours. This, too, might possibly suggest the arrangements of a seraglio, but it would have been quite unfair to deduce, as some of the Old Servants of the Corporation occasionally did, that the RP Junior Temporary Assistants had no other duties. On the contrary, they were in anxious charge of the five thousand recordings in use every week. Those which the Department processed went into the Sound Archives of the war, while the scrap was silent for ever.

'I can't see what good it would be if Mr Brooks did talk to me,' said Lise, who had only been recruited three days earlier, 'I don't know anything.'

Vi replied that it was hard on those in positions of responsibility, like RPD, if they didn't drink, and didn't go to confession.

'Are you a Catholic then?'

'No, but I've heard people say that.'

Vi herself had only been at BH for six months, but since she was getting on for nineteen she was frequently asked to explain things to those who knew even less.

'I daresay you've got it wrong,' she added, being patient with Lise, who was pretty, but shapeless, crumpled and depressed. 'He won't jump on you, it's only a matter of listening.'

'Hasn't he got a secretary?'

'Yes, Mrs Milne, but she's an Old Servant.'

Even after three days, Lise could understand this.

'Or a wife? Isn't he married?'

'Of course he's married. He lives in Streatham, he has a nice home on Streatham Common. He doesn't get back there much, none of the higher grades do. It's non-stop for them, it seems.'

'Have you ever seen Mrs Brooks?'

'No.'

'How do you know his home is nice, then?'

Vi did not answer, and Lise turned the information she had been given so far slowly over in her mind.

'He sounds like a selfish shit to me.'

'I've told you how it is, he thinks people under twenty are more receptive. I don't know why he thinks that. He just tries pouring out his worries to all of us in turn.'

'Has he poured them out to Della?'

'Well, perhaps not Della.'

'What happens if you're not much good at listening? Does he get rid of you?'

Vi explained that some of the girls had asked for transfers because they wanted to be Junior Programme Engineers, who helped with the actual transmissions. That hadn't been in any way the fault of RPD. Wishing that she didn't have to explain matters which would only become clear, if at all, through experience, she checked her watch with the wall clock. An extract from the Prime Minister was wanted for the mid-day news, 1'42" in, cue *Humanity, rather than legality, must be our guide.*

'By the way, he'll tell you that your face reminds him of another face he's seen somewhere – an elusive type of beauty, rather elusive anyway, it might have been a picture somewhere or other, or a photograph, or some-

8

thing in history, or something, but anyway he can't quite place it.'

Lise seemed to brighten a little.

'Won't he ever remember?'

'Sometimes he appeals to Mrs Milne, but she doesn't know either. No, his memory lets him down at that point. But he'll probably put you on the Department's Indispensable Emergency Personnel List. That's the people he wants close to him in case of invasion. We'd be besieged, you see, if that happened. They're going to barricade both ends of Langham Place. If you're on the list you'd transfer then to the Defence Rooms in the sub-basement and you can draw a standard issue of towel, soap and bedding for the duration. Then there was a memo round about hand grenades.'

Lise opened her eyes wide and let the tears slide out, without looking any less pretty. Vi, however, was broadminded, and overlooked such things.

'My boy's in the Merchant Navy,' she said, perceiving the real nature of the trouble. 'What about yours?'

'He's in France, he's with the French army. He *is* French.'

'That's not so good.'

Their thoughts moved separately to what must be kept out of them, helpless waves of flesh against metal and salt water. Vi imagined the soundless fall of a telegram through the letter-box. Her mother would say it was just the same as last time but worse because in those days people seemed more human somehow and the postman was a real friend and knew everyone on his round.

'What's his name, then?'

'Frédé. I'm partly French myself, did they tell you?'

'Well, that can't be helped now.' Vi searched for the right consolation. 'Don't worry if you get put on the IEP list. You won't stay there long. It keeps changing.'

Mrs Milne rang down. 'Is Miss Bernard there? Have I the name correct by the way? We're becoming quite a League of Nations. As she is new to the Department, RPD would like to see her for a few minutes when she comes off shift.'

'We haven't even gone on yet.'

Mrs Milne was accustomed to relax a little with Vi.

'We're having a tiresome day, all these directives, why can't they leave us to go quietly on with our business which we know like the back of our hand. Tell Miss Bernard not to worry about her evening meal, I've been asked to see to a double order of sandwiches.' Lise was not listening, but recalled Vi to the point she had understood best.

'If Mr Brooks says he thinks I'm beautiful, will he mean it?'

'He means everything he says at the time.'

There was always time for conversations of this kind, and of every kind, at Broadcasting House. The very idea of Continuity, words and music succeeding each other without a break except for a cough or a shuffle or some mistake eagerly welcomed by the indulgent public, seemed to affect everyone down to the humblest employee, the filers of Scripts as Broadcast and the fillers-up of glasses of water, so that all in turn could be seen forming close groups, in the canteen, on the seven floors of corridors, beside the basement ticker-tapes, in the washrooms, in the studios, talking, talking to each other, and usually about each other, until the very last moment when the notice SILENCE: ON THE AIR forbade.

The gossip of the seven decks increased the resemblance of the great building to a liner, which the designers had always intended. BH stood headed on a fixed course south. With the best engineers in the world, and a crew varying between the intensely respectable and the barely sane, it looked ready to scorn any disaster of less than Titanic scale. Since the outbreak of war damp sandbags had lapped it round, but once inside the bronze doors, the airs of cooking from the deep hold suggested more strongly than ever a cruise on the Queen Mary. At night, with all its blazing portholes blacked out, it towered over a flotilla of taxis, each dropping off a speaker or two.

By the spring of 1940 there had been a number of castaways. During the early weeks of evacuation Variety, Features and Drama had all been abandoned in distant parts of the country, while the majestic headquarters was left to utter wartime instructions, speeches, talks and news.

Since March the lifts below the third floor had been halted as an economy measure, so that the first three staircases became yet another meeting place. Few nowadays were ever to be found in their offices. An instinct, or perhaps a rapidly acquired characteristic, told the employees how to find each other. On the other hand, in this constant circulation much was lost. The corridors were full of talks producers without speakers, speakers without scripts, scripts which by a clerical error contained the wrong words or no words at all. The air seemed alive with urgency and worry.

Recordings, above all, were apt to be mislaid. They looked alike, all 78s, aluminium discs coated on one side with acetate whose pungent rankness was the true smell of the BBC's war. It was rumoured that the Germans were able to record on tapes coated with ferrous oxide and that this idea might have commercial possibilities in the future, but only the engineers and RPD himself believed this.

'It won't catch on,' the office supervisor told Mrs Milne. 'You could never get attached to them.'

'That's true,' Mrs Milne said. 'I loved my record of Charles Trenet singing *J'ai ta main*. I died the death when it fell into the river at Henley. The public will never get to feel like that about lengths of tape.'

But the Department's discs, though cared for and filed under frequently changing systems, were elusive. Urgently needed for news programmes, they went astray in transit to the studio. Tea-cups were put down on them, and they melted. Ferried back by mobile units through the bitter cold, they froze, and had to be gently restored to life.

11

Hardly a day passed without one or two of them dis-
appearing.

Vi was now looking for Churchill's *Humanity, rather than
legality, must be our guide* with the faint-hearted help of
Lise. It was possible that Lise might turn out to be hopeless.
They'd given up For Transmission, and were looking in what
was admittedly the wrong place, among the Processed,
whose labels, written in the RPAs' round school-leavers'
handwriting, offered First Day of War: Air-Raid Siren, False
Alarm: Cheerful Voices with Chink of Tea-Cups: Polish
Refugees in Scotland, National Singing, No Translation.
'You won't find anything in that lot,' said Della, brassily
stalking through, 'that's all Atmosphere.'

'It's wanted in the editing room. Do you think Radio
News Reel went and took it?'

'Why don't you ask the boys?'

Three of the Junior RPAs were boys, and RPD, though fond
of them, felt less need to confide in them. As the Department
expanded more and more girls would be taken on. 'What a
field that's going to give us!' said Teddy, relaxing in the
greasy haze of the canteen with Willie Sharpe. Willie only
paid twopence for his coffee, because he was a juvenile.

'I don't grudge you that in any way,' Teddy went on. 'It's a
mere accident of birth. I just wonder how you reconcile it
with what you're always saying, that you expect to be in
training as a Spitfire pilot by the end of 1940.'

'My face is changing,' Willie replied. 'Coming up from
Oxford Circus on Wednesday I passed a girl I used to know
and she didn't recognize me.'

Teddy looked at him pityingly.

'They're still asking for School Certificate in maths,' he
said.

'Pretty soon they mayn't mind about that, though. They'll
be taking pilots wherever they can get them.'

'They'll still want people who look a bit more than
twelve.'

Willie was rarely offended, and never gave up.

12

'Hitler was a manual worker, you know. He didn't need School Cert to take command of the Nazi hordes.'

'No, but he can't fly, either,' Teddy pointed out.

The boys' ears, though delicately tuned to differences of pitch and compression, adapted easily to the frightful clash of metal trays in the canteen. Unlike the administrative staff, they had no need to shout. Teddy sat with his back to the counter, so that he could see the girls as they came in – Della, perhaps, although there was nothing doing there – and at the same time turned the pages of a yank mag, where white skin and black lace glimmered. These mags were in short supply. Vi's merchant seaman, who was on the Atlantic run, had passed it on.

'You know, Willie, I need money for what I want to do. Honestly, the kind of woman I have in mind is unattainable on £378 a year.'

'Your mind's tarnished, Teddy.'

'I'm not responsible for more than one eighth of it,' Teddy protested.

'No, but you can increase the proportion by concentrated will-power. As I see it, in any case, after the conflict is over we shan't be at the mercy of anything artificially imposed on us, whether from within or without. Hunger will be a thing of the past because the human race won't tolerate it, mating will follow an understandable instinct, and there'll be no deference to rank or money. We shall need individuals of strong will then.'

Neither Teddy nor anyone else felt that Willie was ridiculous when he spoke like this, although they sometimes wondered what would become of him. Indeed, he was noble. His notebook contained, besides the exact details of his shift duties, a new plan for the organisation of humanity. Teddy also had a notebook, the back of which he kept for the estimated measurements of the Seraglio.

'I'd put this Lise Bernard at 34, 25, 38. Are you with me?'

'I'm not too sure,' said Willie doubtfully. 'By the way, she cries rather a lot.'

'She's mixed a lot with French people, that would make her more emotional.'

'Not all foreigners are emotional. It depends whether they come from the north or the south. Look at Tad.'

Taddeus Zagorski, the third of the junior RPAs (male), had arrived in this country with his parents only last October. How had he managed to learn English so quickly, and how, although he wasn't much older than the rest of them and was quite new to the Department, did he manage to dazzle them with his efficiency and grasp?

'I can't seem to get to like him,' said Teddy. 'He's suffered, I know, but there it is. He wants to be a news reader, you know.'

'I daresay he'll get on,' Willie replied, 'in the world, that is, as it's at present constituted. It's possible that we're jealous of him. We ought to guard against that.'

Tad, in fact, was emerging at the head of the counter queue, where, with a proud gesture, he stirred his coffee with the communal spoon tied to the cash register with a piece of string. He must have been doing Messages From The Forces.

'My auntie got one of those messages,' said Willie. 'It was my uncle in the Navy singing *When the Deep Purple Falls*, but by the time it went out he was missing, believed killed.'

'Was she upset?'

'She never really heard it. She works on a delivery van.'

The young Pole stood at their table, cup of coffee in hand, brooding down at them from a height.

'You should have been off ten minutes ago,' said Teddy.

Tad sat down between them, precisely in the middle of his chair, in his creaseless white shirt. The boys felt uneasy. He had an air of half-suppressed excitement.

'Who is that fellow?' he asked suddenly.

Willie looked up, Teddy craned round. A man with a pale, ruined-looking face was walking up to the bar.

Tad watched him as he asked quietly for a double whisky. The barman seemed unnerved. In fact, the canteen

14

had only obtained a licence at the beginning of the year, on the understanding that the news readers should not take more than two glasses of beer before reporting for work, and the shadow of disapproval still hung over it. Higher grades were expected to go to the Langham for a drink, but this one hadn't.

'I ask you about that fellow,' said Tad, 'because it was he who just came into Studio LG14. I was clearing up the Messages preparatory to returning them to registry, and I asked him what he was doing in the studios, as one cannot be too careful in the present circumstances. He replied that he had an administrative post in the BBC, and, as he seemed respectable, I explained the standard routine to him. I think one should never be too busy to teach those who are anxious to learn.'

'Well, you set out to impress him,' said Teddy. 'What did you tell him?'

'I told him the rules of writing a good news talk – "the first sentence must interest, the second must inform." Next I pointed out the timeless clock, which is such an unusual feature of our studios, and demonstrated the "ten seconds from now".'

The familiar words sounded dramatic, and even tragic. 'What did he do?'

'He nodded, and showed interest.'

'But didn't he say anything?'

'Quite quietly. He said "tell me more."'

Tad's self-assurance wavered and trembled. 'He does not look quite the same now as he did then. Who is he?'

'That's Jeffrey Haggard,' Willie said. 'He's the Director of Programme Planning.'

Tad was silent for a moment. 'Then he would be familiar with the ten second cue?'

'He invented it. It's called the Haggard cue, or the Jeff, sometimes.' Teddy laughed, louder than the din of crockery.

'God, Tad, you've made me happy today. Jeepers Creepers, you've gone and explained the ten second cue to DPP . . .'

15

Their table rocked and shook, while Tad sat motionless, steadying his cup with his hand.

'Doubtless Mr Haggard will think me ludicrous.'

'He thinks everything's ludicrous,' said Willie hastily.

Teddy laughed and laughed, not able to get over it, meaning no harm. He wouldn't laugh like that if he was Polish, Willie thought. However, in his scheme of things to come there would no frontiers, and indeed no countries.

The Director of Programme Planning ordered a second double in his dry, quiet, disconcerting voice. Probably in the whole of his life he had never had to ask for anything twice. The barman, knowing, as most people did, that Mr Haggard had run through three wives and had lost his digestion into the bargain, wondered what he'd sound like if he got angry.

The whisky, though it had no visible effect, was exactly calculated to raise DPP from a previous despair far enough to face the rest of the evening. When he had finished it he went back to his office, where he managed with no secretary and very few staff, and rang RPD.

'Mrs Milne, I want Sam. I can hear him shouting, presumably in the next room.'

On the telephone his voice dropped even lower, like a voice's shadow. He waited, looking idly at the schedules that entirely covered the walls, the charts of Public Listening and Evening Meal Habits, and the graphs, supplied by the Ministry of Information, of the nation's morale.

RPD was put through.

'Jeff, I want you to hear my case.'

DDP had been hearing it for more than ten years. But, to do his friend justice, it was never the same twice running. The world seemed new created every day for Sam Brooks, who felt no resentment and, indeed, very little recollection of what he had suffered the day before.

'Jeff, Establishment have hinted that I'm putting in for too many girls.'

'How can that be?'

'They know I like to have them around, they know I

need that. I've drafted a reply, saying nothing, mind you, about the five thousand discs a week, or the fact that we provide a service to every other department of the Corporation. See what you think of the way I've put it – I begin quite simply, by asking them whether they realize that through the skill of the recording engineer sound can be transformed from air to wax, the kind of thing which through all the preceding centuries has been possible only to the bees. It's the transference of pattern, you see – surely that says something encouraging about the human mind. Don't forget that Mozart composed that trio while he was playing a game of billiards.'

'Sam, I went to a meeting to-day.'

'What about?'

'It was about the use of recordings in news bulletins.'

'Why wasn't I asked?'

But Sam was never asked to meetings.

'We had two Directors and three Ministries – War, Information, Supply. They'd called it, quite genuinely I think, in the interests of truth.'

The word made its mark. Broadcasting House was in fact dedicated to the strangest project of the war, or of any war, that is, telling the truth. Without prompting, the BBC had decided that truth was more important than consolation, and, in the long run, would be more effective. And yet there was no guarantee of this. Truth ensures trust, but not victory, or even happiness. But the BBC had clung tenaciously to its first notion, droning quietly on, at intervals from dawn to midnight, telling, as far as possible, exactly what happened. An idea so unfamiliar was bound to upset many of the other authorities, but they had got used to it little by little, and the listeners had always expected it.

'The object of the meeting was to cut down the number of recordings in news transmissions – in the interests of truth, as they said. The direct human voice must be used whenever we can manage it – if not, the public must be clearly told what they've been listening to – the programme must be announced as recorded, that is, Not Quite Fresh.'

Sam's Department was under attack, and with it every recording engineer, every RPA, every piece of equipment, every TD7, mixer and fader and every waxing and groove in the building. As the protector and defender of them all, he became passionate.

'Did they give specific instances? Could they even find one?'

'They started with Big Ben. It's always got to be relayed direct from Westminster, the real thing, never from disc. That's got to be firmly fixed in the listeners' minds. Then, if Big Ben is silent, the public will know that the war has taken a distinctly unpleasant turn.'

'Jeff, the escape of Big Ben freezes in cold weather.'

'We shall have to leave that to the Ministry of Works.'

'And the King's stammer. Ah, what about that. My stand-by recordings for his speeches to the nation – His Majesty without stammer, in case of emergency.'

'Above all, not those.'

'And Churchill. . . .'

'Some things have to go, that was decided at a preliminary talk long before I got there. Otherwise it's just a general directive, and we've lived through a good many of those. It doesn't affect the total amount of recording. If you want to overwork, you've nothing to worry about.' Sam said that he accepted that no-one present had had the slightest under-standing of his Department's work, but it was strange, very strange, that there had been no attempt whatever, at any stage, to consider his point of view.

'If someone could have reasoned with him, Jeff. Perhaps this idea that's come to me about the bees. . . .'

'I protested against any cuts in your mobile recording units. I managed to save your cars.'

'Those Wolseleys!'

'They're all you've got, Sam.'

'The hearses. I've been asking for replacements for two years. They're just about fit to take a Staff Officer to a lunch party, wait till he collapses from over-indulgence, then on to the graveyard. And I've had to send two of those out to France. . . . Jeff, were you asked to break this to me?'

'In a way.' As they left the meeting one of the Directors had drawn him aside and had asked him to avoid mentioning the new recommendations to RPD for as long as possible.

Sam was floundering in his newly acquired wealth of grievances.

'Without even the commonplace decency . . . no standbys . . . my cars, well, I suppose you did your best there . . . my girls. . . .'

'In my opinion you can make do with the staff you've got,' Jeff said. 'One of your RPAs was talking to me in the studio just now, and I assure you he was very helpful.'

When he had done what he could Jeff walked out of the building. It was scarcely necessary for him to show his pass. His face, with its dark eyebrows, like a comedian's, but one who had to be taken seriously, was the best known in the BBC. He stood for a moment among the long shadows on the pavement, between the piles of sandbags which had begun to rot and grow grass, now that spring had come.

DPP was homeless, in the sense of having several homes, none of which he cared about more than the others. There was a room he could use at the Langham, and then there were two or three women with whom his relationship was quite unsentimental, but who were not sorry to see him when he came. He never went to his house, because his third wife was still in it. In any case, he had a taxi waiting for him every night, just round the corner in Riding House Street. He hardly ever used it, but it was a testimony that if he wanted to, he could get away quickly.

RPD seemed to have forgotten how to go home. Mrs Milne suggested as much to him as she said goodnight. Her typewriter slumbered now under its leatherette cover. He gave no sign of having heard her.

Long before it was dark men in brown overalls went round BH, fixing the framed blackouts in every window, circulating in the opposite direction to the Permanents coming downstairs, while the news readers moved laterally to check with Pronunciation, pursued by editors bringing later messages on pink cards. Movement was complex, so too was time. Nobody's hour of work coincided exactly with the life-cycle of Broadcasting House, whose climax came six times in the twenty-four hours with the Home News, until at nine o'clock, when the nation sat down to listen, the building gathered its strength and struck. The night world was crazier than the day world. When Lise Bernard paused in doubt at the door of RPD's office, she saw her Head of Department pacing to and fro like a bear astray, in a grove of the BBC's pale furniture, veneered with Empire woods. He wore a tweed jacket, grey trousers and one of the BBC's frightful house ties, dark blue embroidered with thermionic valves in red. Evidently he put on whatever came to hand first. Much of the room was taken up with a bank of turntables and a cupboard full of clean shirts.

When he recognized who she was he stopped pacing about and took off his spectacles, changing from a creature of sight to one of faith. Lise, the crowded office, the neatly angled sandwiches, the tray with its white cloth suitable for grades of Director and above, turned into patches of light and shade. To Lise, on the other hand, looking at his large hazel eyes, the eyes of a child determined not to blink for fear of missing something, he became someone who could not harm her and asked to be protected from harm. The effect, however, was quite unplanned, he produced it unconsciously. All the old lechers and yearners in the building envied the success which he seemed to turn to so little account.

'He just weeps on their shoulders you know,' they said. 'And yet I believe the man's a trained engineer.'

'Sit down, Miss Bernard. Have all these sandwiches. You look hungry.' When he had put his spectacles on again he couldn't pursue this idea; Lise was decidedly overweight. 'I like to get to know everyone who comes to work for me as soon as possible – in a way it's part of the responsibility I feel for all of you – and the shortest way to do that, curiously enough, I've found, is to tell you some of the blankly incomprehensible bloody idiotic lack of understanding that our Department meets with every minute of the day.'

Lise sat there blankly, eating nothing. He picked up the telephone, sighing.

'Canteen, I have a young assistant here, quite new to the Corporation, who can't eat your sandwiches.'

'That's National Cheese, Mr Brooks. The manufacturers have agreed to amalgamate their brand names for the duration in the interest of the Allied war effort.'

'I believe you've been waiting to say that all day.'

'I don't want anything, Mr Brooks, really I don't,' whimpered Lise.

'Not good enough for you.' He looked angrily at the window, unable to throw them out because of the blackout. Then he sat down opposite to the girl and considered her closely. 'You know, even though I only saw you for a few minutes at the interview, I was struck by the width between your eyes. You can see something like it in those portraits by – I'm sure you know the ones I mean. It's a sure index of a certain kind of intelligence, I would call it an emotional intelligence.' Lise wished that there was a looking-glass in the room.

'Some people might find what I have to say difficult to grasp, because I let my ideas follow each other just as they come. But people whose eyes are as wide apart as yours won't have that difficulty.' He took her hand, but held it quite absent-mindedly.

'You may find Broadcasting House rather strange at first, but there's nothing unusual about me. Except for this, I suppose – it just so happens that all my energies are concentrated, and always have been, and always will be, on one thing, the recording of sound and of the human

21

voice. That doesn't make for an easy life, you understand. Perhaps you know what it's like to have a worry that doesn't and can't leave room in your mind for anything else and won't give you peace, night or day, for a single moment.'

Now something went not at all according to programme. Lise began to sob. These tears were not of her usual manageable kind, and her nose turned red. Having no handkerchief with her she struggled to her feet and heaved and streamed her way out of the room.

'Bad news?' asked Teddy, meeting her in the corridor. Set on her way to the Ladies, she only shook her head. RPD's gone for one of them at last, he thought. Jeez, I don't blame him. But Della, expert in human behaviour, thought this impossible.

'Why?' Teddy asked. 'He's capable.'

'If it was that, she wouldn't be crying.'

When Lise did not come back, Sam was at first mildly puzzled, and then forgot about her. But he was still oppressed with the injustice that had been done to him in the name of truth, in the name of patriotism too, if you thought of the cheese sandwiches, and the added injustice of being abandoned without a listener. In the end he had to turn to Vi, too busy and perhaps too accustomed to his ways to be quite what he wanted, but not tearful, and always reliable. By this time, however, having been sorting out administrative and technical problems since five in the morning, he was exhausted. He put his head on her shoulder, as he was always rumoured to do, took off his spectacles, and went to sleep immediately.

Twenty minutes passed. It was coming up for the nine o'clock news.

'Aren't you exceeding your duties?' said one of the recording engineers, putting his head round the door. 'You've got a situation on your hands there.'

'If that's a name for cramp,' said Vi.

2

The second year of the war was not a time when the staff of BH gave very much thought to promotion. But, even so, it seemed odd that Jeff Haggard and Sam Brooks, who, though they could hardly be termed Old Servants, had been bitterly loyal for more than ten years, should be nothing more than DPP and RPD. True, nobody else could have done their jobs, and then again Sam always seemed too overworked to notice, and Jeff too detached to care. One might have assumed that they would be there for ever.

But if they were either to move or to leave, it would have to be together. Without understanding either their warmly unreasonable RPD, or their sardonic DPP, the BBC knew that for a fact. The link between them was consolingly felt as the usefulness of having Haggard around when Brooks had to be got out of trouble. This was enough for practical purposes, but Jeff would have liked to have been able to explain it further. By nature he was selfish. He had left his first wife because he had found his second wife more attractive, and his second wife had left him because, as she told her lawyers, she could never make him raise his voice. It was, therefore, going against his nature, a most unsafe proceeding, to put himself out to help a friend, worse still to do so for so long. Their long relationship looked like an addiction – a weakness for the weak on Jeff's part – or a response to the appeal for protection made by the defenceless and single-minded. Of course, if this appeal were to fail entirely, the human race would have difficulty in reproducing itself.

Perhaps if Sam had ever been able to foresee the result of his actions, or if he had suspected for one moment that he was not entirely self-sufficient, the spell might have been broken, or perhaps there was a fixed point in the past when that might have been done.

'I ought to have stopped in 1938,' Jeff thought. 'With Englishry.' At the time of the Munich Agreement a memo had been sent round calling, as a matter of urgency, for the recording of our country's heritage.

It was headed *Lest we forget our Englishry*. Sam had disappeared for over two weeks in one of the Wolseleys, pretty infirm even at that time, with an engineer and an elderly German refugee, Dr Vogel – Dr Vogel, cruelly bent, deaf in one ear, but known to be the greatest expert in Europe on recorded atmosphere.

There was not much hope of commonsense prevailing. Dr Vogel, in spite of his politeness and gentle *ganz meinerheits*, was an obsessive, who had been seen to take the arms of passers-by in his bony grip and beg to record their breathing, for he wished to record England's wheezing before the autumn fogs began. 'Have the goodness, sir, to cough a little into my apparatus.' Sam thought the idea excellent.

The expedition to the English countryside arrived back with a very large number of discs. The engineer who had gone with them said nothing. He went straight away to have a drink. It was probably a misfortune that the Controllers were so interested in the project that they demanded a playback straight away. Usually there was a judicious interval before they expressed any opinion, but not this time.

'What we have been listening to – patiently, always in the hope of something else coming up – amounts to more than six hundred bands of creaking. To be accurate, some are a mixture of squeaking and creaking.'

'They're all from the parish church of Hither Lickington,' Sam explained eagerly. 'It was recommended to us by Religious Broadcasting as the top place in the Home Counties. What you're hearing is the hinges of the door and the door itself opening and shutting as the old women come in one by one with the stuff for the Harvest Festival. The quality's superb, particularly on the last fifty-three bands or so. Some of them have got more to carry, so the door has to open wider. That's when you get the squeak.'

'Hark, the vegetable marrow comes!' cried Dr Vogel, his head on one side, well contented.

For several weeks the Recorded Programme Department was in danger of complete reorganization, for the BBC could form and re-form its elements with ease. It was put to DPP, in consultation, that although RPD was successfully in charge of hundreds of thousands of pounds' worth of equipment, and no fault could be found with his technical standing. . . .

'You feel that he's too interested in creaking doors,' Jeff said.

'He's irresponsible.'

'Oh, I wouldn't say so.'

'There was a considerable financial investment in this project, and Brooks was well aware that copies of the recordings were to be buried certain fathoms in the earth as a memorial for future generations.'

'You could still do that,' Jeff replied. 'There mayn't be any doors that creak by then. Mine doesn't now.' All the doors in BH were fitted with self-closing devices of an irritating nature.

It was not Jeff's habit to soothe, but as usual the case he made for his friend, only just over the borderline of detachment, and gradually becoming more serious, proved effective. Sam never heard of these discussions. He continued like a sleepwalker, who never knows what obstacles are removed, and by what hands, from his path.

And Sam was not the only member of the Corporation who confided in Jeff. That was surprising, in view of the imperturbable surface he presented, which gave back only a stony resonance, truthful and dry, to the complaints of others. But his advice was excellent, and he could be relied

25

upon, as so few could, not to wait for a convenient opening to start on his own grievances. Perhaps he hadn't any, certainly he admitted to none. His calmness was really recklessness, as of a gambler who no longer felt anything was valuable enough to stake. That in turn was not likely to make him popular. Those who valued his cold judgement when they needed it, very naturally resented it when they didn't. To see the Director of Programme Planning miscalculate might have been a relief, but during the first nine months of the war no hint of such a thing arose – never, until the affair of General Pinard.

'You'll get your boy back, then,' said Della to Lise. A strong line was best, in her opinion. Everyone knew that Lise considered herself engaged and that Frédé was some kind of electrician with the French 1st Army. The way things were going they'd have to bring the French over here, there was nowhere else for them to go.

'But that will be quite impossible,' said Tad, demonstrating with his map. 'You underestimate the obstacle of the English Channel.'

'In that case, if you want my advice, you'd do best to forget him,' said Della. 'After all, he never gave you a ring, did he?'

Lise had not proved any better at her work than Della, which made some sort of bond between them.

Vi's merchant seaman wrote making apparent references to home leave, but a good deal of his letter had been blacked out by the censor. What a job having to go through other people's personal letters, Vi thought, they must feel uncomfortable, you had to pity them.

On June 10 1940 the French Government admitted that Paris could not be defended, and left for Bordeaux. Between the *débandade* and de Gaulle's arrival on the 17th, there was a bizarre moment of hope when the Government learned that General Georges Pinard had escaped to London, flying his own light aircraft, and bringing with him nothing but a small valise and one junior officer. He went straight to the Rembrandt Hotel.

Historians have not yet decided – or rather, they have decided but not agreed – as to who sent the General on his desperate mission. Certainly no-one could have been more welcome. Whereas de Gaulle was practically unknown in Britain, Pinard was instantly recognizable, with his coarse silvery moustache, the joy of worn-out cartoonists, and his nose broken by a fall from a horse and flattened out of its French sharpness. His name was one of the few that the public knew well and it created its own picture.

The General was a peasant's son from the flattest, wettest and most unpicturesque part of France, where the provinces of Aisne and Somme join. Born in 1869, he grew up with the Prussian occupation; the army rescued him from hoeing root vegetables, and he rose at a moderate speed through the ranks. Improbable as it seemed, he was a romantic, a Dreyfusard and a devotee of the aeroplane – indeed, his lectures on the importance of airpower delayed his promotion by several years. However, he cared nothing for Empire, nothing for impossible ambitions, only for the stubborn defence of the solid earth of his country. In the Great War, he was with one of the only two divisions not affected by the mutiny of 1917. He always slept excellently, and it was said that he had to be wakened by his orderly before every battle.

When the Ecole Supérieure de Guerre was reopened in 1919, Pinard was one of the first to be appointed, and was looked upon as a sound man, a counterweight, with his peasant blood, to the impossible de Gaulle. In 1940, in spite of his advanced age, he had managed to get himself the command of the 5th Armoured Division, which, in the middle of May, had made a last counterattack against the German advance.

A romantic, then, though limited by earth and sky, but nothing in his military career explained his curious fondness for the English. This could be traced to his shrewd marriage with a very rich woman, addicted, as

27

Pinard was himself, to racehorses. Between the wars he had become a familiar figure at bloodstock sales, and at Epsom and Ascot. Much photographed at every meeting, he was always cheerful, and most important of all, nearly always a loser. That was the foundation of his great popularity over here, something he had never attained in France. On his wife's money, he became an Anglophile. He learnt to love because he was loved, for the first time in his life.

At half-past eight on the 14th of June the Director General's office told DPP that General Pinard was going on the air as soon as it could be arranged. 'He wants to broadcast to the English nation and it seems it's a matter of great urgency. It's all been agreed.'

'Well, the evening programmes must shove over a bit,' said Jeff. 'I'll see to it.'

'It's more than that. We want you down in the studio.'

'What for?'

'Don't you speak fluent French?'

'Well?'

'He wants you there when Pinard comes.'

'He speaks perfectly good English, with a strong French accent, which is exactly what you want.'

'The point is this – the War Office is sending someone and so is the F.O., and the DG and DDG don't think it will look well if we can't produce a French speaker from our top level in BH.'

'What do you want me to say?'

'Oh, it might be a few sentences of greeting. Some hospitality may be considered appropriate. I suppose there'd better be some absinthe, isn't that what they drink?'

'The General prefers cognac,' Jeff said.

'Have you met him, then? That might be extremely useful.'

'I met him in a dugout, behind a village called Quesnoy en Santerre, twenty-three years ago.'

'I've never heard you talk about your war experiences before, Haggard.'

'This wasn't an experience. We were supposed to be taking over from the French, then it turned out that we were retreating. I was Mess Officer and I stayed to see if the French had left any brandy behind, they did sometimes. Pinard came back with exactly the same idea in mind. He was a captain then. I don't flatter myself that he'll remember this incident, by the way.'

'I see, well, that isn't really . . . did he seem to be a good speaker?'

'He didn't say very much on that occasion.'

'In a sense it hardly matters whether he is or not. It's a morale talk, he's expected to fly on to Morocco to organize the resistance there, he'll want to encourage himself as well as us.'

General Pinard arrived brushed and shining, to the relief of the Talks Producer, who believed, in the old way, that appearances were projected through the microphone. His silent young aide wished to accompany him into the studio, but was detained in the rather crowded continuity room. Pinard sat down behind the glass panel, his eyes resting for a moment upon everybody present.

'He won't wear headphones,' the Talks Producer told Jeff. 'It seems he doesn't like them. He prefers to go ahead on a hand cue.'

'I don't think we should grudge him anything.'

The canteen's brandy, Martell 2 Star, left over from Christmas, was brought out. The General raised his hand in a gesture of mild, but emphatic, refusal. That meant that no-one could have any – a disappointment to everybody except Talks, whose allocation for the month had already run out. The brandy would now do for the Minister of Coastal Defence, due later that evening. But these considerations faded as the General's presence was felt. He waited in immaculate dignity. Behind him lay France's broken armies.

A piece of paper was put in front of him. He looked at it, then moved it to one side.

In the continuity studio it was hardly possible to move. The War Office's Major, the Foreign Office's liaison man, sat awkwardly on high stools. The young French aide stood warily on guard. The Acting Deputy Director General suddenly came in through the soundless door to join them. DPP leant in a corner, looking up at the ceiling.

'Don't forget it's your duty to put everyone at their ease,' he said to the talks producer.

'He didn't look at my notes and suggestions. We need a run-through.'

'You've no time. I did what I could for you, but we can't alter the nine o'clock. You're on in forty-three seconds.'

The producer pressed his switch.

'How would you like to be introduced, General?'

'I don't know,' Pinard replied. 'I am in uniform, but I am a soldier without a post, an officer without authority, and a Frenchman without a country.'

'The English people know your name quite well, sir.'

'Use it if you wish. But make it clear that I am speaking to them as an individual. I have something to say from the heart.'

'How long is this going to take?' asked the programme engineer. No-one knew, it was open-ended. The PE's face tightened with disapproval.

'My dear friends,' General Pinard said, 'many persons who have occupied the stage of history have been forgiven not only their mistakes, but their sins, because of what they did at one moment only. I pray that for me, this will prove to be the moment.'

It was a quiet, moving, old man's voice, with a slight metallic edge.

'It gives me a strange feeling to speak to you this evening, and even stranger, after all that has happened in the past few weeks, to think that I should be speaking the truth, and that so many of you should be willing to hear it. Old soldiers like to tell stories, and old generals most of all. That kind of story is called a *giberne*.'

30

The producer passed a note: *should we translate at the end?* ADDG wrote: *I think a few untranslated French words give the right atmosphere.* Jeff wrote: *don't worry, he's not going to tell it anyway.*

'This evening I am not here to indulge myself with a *giberne*. I have come to tell you what I saw yesterday, and what you must do tomorrow.

'But perhaps you will say to yourselves, "I am listening to a Frenchman." He is French, and I am English and I don't trust him, any more than I would have done these past five hundred years, let them make what alliances they will. And today above all I don't trust him, this evening I don't trust him, because his country has been defeated. You know that every road leading to the south is impassable, every road is crowded not only with troops in retreat, but with families on the move, the old, the weak and the very young, the bedding, the cooking-pots, the scenes to which we have become so terribly accustomed since Poland fell.'

'What's this about cooking-pots?' said the engineer to his JPE. 'He may be going to break down. Watch the level.'

'So, to repeat, you will think: I shan't trust this man. . . . And we French, do we trust the English? The answer is: not at all. In the past weeks, most of all in the past twenty-four hours, I have heard you called many hard names, I don't only mean by colleagues in the Conseil de Guerre but every soldier and every little shopkeeper on the road. They say that you led us unprepared into war with Germany and that having done so you have deserted us. And perhaps "in the misfortunes of our friends there is something not displeasing to us". Well, in that case you must be satisfied. We are ruined, and we blame it on you.

'Why then when I began to speak to you did I call you "friends"? That is a word that means so much that I understand no language is without it. I use it to you, and I mean it. The truth is that I am here this evening, in spite of all I have said, because I care deeply for England and the English.

31

'Well, is this nonsense, or is the old man weak in the head? No more unsuitable task could be imagined than for a general, worse still, an aged general, to show his feelings. And those who hold power in France at the moment did not wish me to come. They tried to prevent me, but I came.'

Without warning, General Pinard's voice rose to the level of the parade ground, and the engineer, caught on the hop, allowed it to blast fifteen million listeners.

'But, believe me, I am not here to flatter you! That would not be the duty of friendship. Dear listeners, dear Englishmen and women, dear people of the green fields, the streets and the racecourses that I know so well – I have seen my nation lose hope, and I say to you now that there is no hope for you either, *ne vous faîtes pas aucune illusion*, you have lost your war. I tell you – do not listen to your leaders – neither those who are ready, as they always have been, to depart from these shores to Canada, nor to the courageous drunkard whom you have made your Prime Minister.'

The talks producer stared round from face to face, his hand on the censor switch, waiting for orders. The Foreign Office confronted the War Office.

'Who's going to stop him?'

'I don't know who authorized him to speak. I understand it was the War Cabinet.'

'I'll get on to the PM's office,' said the Assistant Deputy Director General.

'Don't barricade yourselves in, dear English people, do not take down your rusty shotguns. The French are a nation who have always cared about their army, while you have never cared about yours. Be sure that it won't protect you now, and most certainly you cannot protect yourselves. When the Germans arrive, and at best it will be in a few weeks, don't think of resistance, don't think of history. Nothing is so ungrateful as history. Think of yourselves, your homes and gardens which you tend so carefully, the sums of money you have saved, the children who will live

32

to see all this pass and who will know that all governments are bad, and Hitler's perhaps not worse than any other. I tell you out of affection what France has learnt at the cost of terrible sacrifice. Give in. When you hear the tanks rolling up the streets of your quarter, be ready to give in, no matter how hard the terms. Give in when the Boche comes in. Give in.'

A terrible fit of coughing overwhelmed the microphone.

'He's overloading,' said the programme engineer, in agony.

'*Messieurs, brisons là . . . je crève . . .*'

'What does he mean by that?' asked the producer, unnerved, seizing DPP by the arm.

'What do you think he means?' said Jeff. 'He's not feeling well.' The General's right hand, lying on the table in front of him, opened and shut. He tried to force himself to stay sitting upright, but could not. His face, with its heavy silver moustaches, had turned bluish red.

The young aide was almost in tears. He had remained silent, no French junior officer speaks in the presence of his superior, clearly now he was at the end of his endurance. Jeff, who could move very quickly, picked up the bottle of Martell and taking the aide with him went into the other studio, emptied the BBC's glass of water onto the floor and filled it with brandy for the poor trembling old man. With a very different gesture now, the hand rejected it.

'*Surtout pas ça.*'

The duty officer rang through. There had been many complaints. For the past ten minutes there had been total silence on the Home network. The fifteen million listeners had heard nothing. But their reaction was not surprise so much as a kind of relief, the interruption of their programmes being exactly the kind of thing which everyone had expected from the moment war was declared, but which had failed to happen, holding the listeners' attention in a supersaturated solution which had failed month by month to crystallize. The public put even greater confidence in the BBC, because for ten minutes it had failed to speak to them.

*

'Of course I pulled the plugs on the General,' said Jeff. 'I felt that what he was going to say wouldn't, on the whole, be helpful to the nation at this particular juncture.'

'How in God's name did you know what he was going to say?' ADDG asked, jolted and disturbed to the very depths of his Old Servantship.

'I didn't know. I guessed.'

'I don't get it. He seemed quite all right to me when he arrived.'

'I didn't think so.'

'Why not?'

'It was something he said to me in the corridor, just before he got to the studios.'

'I didn't notice, I came down later.'

'He did recognize me, after all. I ought to have realized that generals always do remember faces, otherwise they don't become generals.'

'What did he say?'

'He said: I am going to repeat my former advice.'

'Meaning what?'

'I told you about the St Quentin front and the cognac. There was plenty left but it wasn't drinkable, it had got mixed up with dead Germans. I was going to see what I could salvage just the same, but Pinard stopped me. He said, "*Soyons réalistes*".'

'And you went ahead, entirely on your own initiative, because of that?'

'It's time to be realistic . . . I thought I'd better be on the safe side.'

'If you call it that. Why in the name of God didn't you consult me? In ordinary circumstances you wouldn't have been in the studio at all. Of course, I admit that as things turned out we've been saved from a very dangerous incident, it might have caused I don't know what despondency and panic, furthermore it would have given the M.O.I. and the War Office exactly the chance they've been looking for to step in and threaten our independence and press for governmental control – I grant you all that, I suppose in a sense one ought to congratulate you, perhaps you're expecting to be congratulated. . . .' He paused. Jeff had never been known to expect anything of the kind. 'Leaving that aside, you acted without authority, and as a member of the administrative staff meddling with the equipment you've risked a strong protest from the unions. I don't know what to say to you. Heads will roll. He was a privileged speaker. Do you intend to do this sort of thing often?'

'I hope we shan't often be within measurable distance of invasion.'

'I don't like that, Haggard.'

'I don't mind withdrawing "measurable".'

ADDG had judged the reactions of the Ministries correctly. No-one, it was true, could deny that to let General Pinard's appeal, so wretched, so heartfelt, go out to the unsuspecting public would have been a setback. Equally, it was no-one's business, now that the General had been taken seriously ill, to decide what kind of a setback it might have been. This left more scope for attack. The BBC, in face of the grave doubts of the Services, who felt the less said the better on every occasion, persisted obstinately in telling the truth in their own way. But their own way was beginning to look irresponsible to the point of giddiness. And if directors of departments were to take a hand in decision-making of this order, what guarantee could there be that other French leaders who might cross the Channel in the hope of continuing the struggle would not be cut off in their turn? This last remark was part of a combined directive from the Ministries, which also suggested a formula: Haggard might be complimented on his presence of mind and packed off to one of the Regions for the duration. A new post could surely be created if necessary.

The BBC loyally defended their own. As a cross between a civil service, a powerful moral force, and an amateur theatrical company that wasn't too sure where next week's money was coming from, they had several different kinds of language, and could guarantee to come out best from almost any discussion. Determined to go on doing what they thought best without official interference, they spoke of their DPP's artistic temperament which could not be restrained without risk, and when asked why they'd put this freakish impresario in charge of planning, they referred to his rigid schedules and steely devotion to duty. Then, after a few days, it became known that the Prime Minister had heard the whole story and thought it was excellent. He'd particularly liked the phrase 'to pull the plugs on someone', which he hadn't, apparently, come across before.

The Pinard affair was closed. But it did nothing to lessen that distance or difference between DPP and some of his colleagues, which they felt as an atmosphere of faint coldness even when they needed his help. Jeff Haggard was useful because if he felt a matter was worth taking up he didn't mind what he said or who he said it too. Look at what he'd done, over the years, for Sam Brooks! Undoubtedly, also, he was clever. But they felt, perhaps out of a sense of self-preservation, that no-one can be good and clever at the same time.

ADDG, with the leniency of someone who has been unjust in the first place, considered that Haggard's nerves might have been overtaxed. The planning of the complete Home and Forces programmes, in all their delicate bearings, couldn't be undertaken with impunity.

'I think I'll advise him to read a few chapters of *Cranford* every night before he retires to bed. I've been doing that myself ever since Munich. I think, you know, that Mrs Gaskell would have been glad to know that.'

The whole notion was comforting, but in fact Jeff had never been nervous and was now arguably the calmest person in the whole building. He didn't regard himself as either lucky, or in disgrace, but, if he was either, the feeling was quite familiar.

On the night of the 16th of June General Pinard died in the King Edward VII Hospital for Officers. It was impossible to send the body back to German-occupied territory and an awkward funeral took place at Notre Dame de France, off Leicester Square. The BBC sent a wreath, with a card on which Jeff had written *À Georges Pinard: mort pour la civilisation.* On the 17th of June de Gaulle arrived in this country.

Like Pinard, he had brought only a small suitcase. He was lodged in the Rubens Hotel and given permission to broadcast and to raise his own army.

There were French sailors camping at Aintree, French airmen in South Wales, two battalions of légionnaires at Tufnell Park, French gunners, chasseurs and signals at Alexandra Park. 'You'll never find him,' Vi said to Lise, 'we'll all do our best, though. What does your family think?' But Lise's father, who had been a cashier at Barclay's Lyons branch, had brought his family back to England in January and was now a cashier in Southampton. He wasn't favourable to the idea of Frédé and never had been.

'Well, does he know your London address?'

Lise wasn't sure, and it wouldn't do anyway. She had a room in a Catholic hostel attached to a convent near Warren Street.

'How do you know he'll turn up at all?' asked Teddy. Lise replied that she was psychic, with the result that she had a certain sensation in the points of her breasts when Frédé was near at hand.

'Who'd be a woman?' Teddy thought.

All this time Lise had remained steadily in low spirits. RPD had made only a half-hearted attempt to tell Mrs Milne that Miss Bernard was very unusual, probably talented, should not on any account be overworked, and so forth. His heart was not in it. She was less responsive than the deadened walls of the studios. But now her sluggish energies seemed to revive, at least to the extent of asking other people to do something for her.

The mobile unit had been sent by Archives to capture

the scene at de Gaulle's new headquarters in Westminster. Here, in a dusty bare room, those who had made the decision to join France Libre signed their names, and afterwards drank a pledge to Victory from a barrel of red wine in the passage. 'Not much of a sound picture there,' said the recording engineer, who had flatly refused to let Dr Vogel accompany him. 'You've just got them taking this oath, footsteps coming and going on the bare boards, a nice bit of echo there, your wine coming out of the tap and a few more words, nothing in English, though.'

'Did you see anyone who looked like a sapper?' Lise asked him with dazed, heavy persistence.

'Search me, sweetheart.'

'He's bound to come there one day. He's sure to want to stay in England.'

'Well, we're going back tomorrow to see if we can get some more atmosphere. With luck, one of them might smash a glass.' The RE told Willie Sharpe that Lise seemed pretty well idiotic. 'You don't make allowances for human hope,' Willie replied.

And yet, out of the two hundred thousand French troops brought over here and quartered at random, in the miraculously fair weather, wherever a space could be found, they did come across Frédé.

They were out for a breather in Kensington Gardens – Della and Vi, with Lise, who had made them go there in the first place, dragging behind. You often saw French soldiers in the gardens, detachments of *français libres* and of the vastly greater number who had not signed on and were waiting to go back home as soon as they got the chance. There wasn't much for them to do in a park, but then, there wasn't much for them to do anyway.

Della never went out looking less than her best. She wore a striped silk blouse with a deeply suggestive V-neckline under her red linen costume; on the lapels of this she pinned, on alternate weeks, her RAF wings, naval crown, Free Polish, Free Czech, Free Norwegian, Free Dutch and Free Belgian flashes and the badges of

Canadian and New Zealand regiments. Her hair was gallantly swept back in sparkling ridges and she advanced on high heels, ready to receive or repel any opening shots in the way of glances, remarks, or hard cheek. Under persuasion, Lise had also bought a pair of strapped high-heeled shoes. Della felt almost professionally insulted at the idea of a friend trying to meet her fiancé, if that was what he was, without tarting herself up at least a little. Vi looked her usual self in a cotton dress she had made on her mother's machine. It was all right, but no more than that.

Kensington's leafy glades were full of lovers and, at a discreet distance, workers off work, each with their own thermos. The girls passed close enough to the anti-aircraft battery to hear and take no apparent notice of the long whistle that followed them. At last they chose to sit on the ground at the edge of the dingle, with a good view of the Peter Pan statue. 'I expect the man who made that died young,' Della said. It was odd for them, after eight hours in BH, to sit on the grass, picking off bits of grass and chewing them, under the lazing clouds.

When the French soldiers appeared they came in two groups, and from opposite directions, a few *français libres* to begin with, idling across from Hyde Park. They stopped at the bridge and looked at the water, not as if they knew each other very well as yet. Someone had given them cigarettes and they had evidently stopped by previous arrangement to hand round the packets and allow them-selves one each. Quite a few of them had légionnaires' chinstrap beards and Della, who had never seen these before, kept pointing. Vi jerked her elbow down. Without a word Lise heaved herself to her feet and began to stumble forward on her strappies, but the other way, towards the Round Pond.

There the summer turf of the gardens was dotted with more French soldiers coming over the ridge, who suddenly all sat or lay down, like a herd on a fine day. They were determined not to go any farther. A refreshment van, driven by a middle-aged woman in a navy-blue beret, pulled up and parked itself among them. On its side you could read, painted in white, the words ANGLO-FRENCH AMENITIES COMMITTEE. She opened up the side of her van and began to count out rolls of bread and paper cups. Nobody took any notice of her.

Lise gracelessly panted up the slope to within speaking distance. A man got to his feet. True, she'd never told them exactly what this Frédé looked like, but this one was short, and not even dark. It was deeply disappointing, and at the same time confusing – Lise made an awkward grab and then lost her footing, then righted herself and clung on to him, taller than he was and much heavier. She seemed to be wrestling with the dishevelled khaki creature.

'I wouldn't have thought she'd got it in her,' said Della. Stir it up, she thought. She only wanted for Lise what she'd have liked for herself.

'Yes but those aren't Free French,' said Vi. 'He's got into the wrong lot.' She was frightened. Against the protests of Frédé and his cronies Lise was crying out in French, and when she did that she seemed to turn into another person, or let out the one she had been all along. This made the girls feel queer.

By now the FLs on the bridge had finished their cigarettes and put the stubs away inside their caps. Sighting the others on the opposite slope only two hundred yards away, they warily advanced through Peter Pan's dingle. Then some of them began to run in ragged formation, like boys anxious to get into a football game, the small, neat and elegant ones in front, as though trained, others in the rear beating up clouds of dust with their boots from the dry earth. Lise and Frédé disappeared from sight as the hostile forces engaged, the front runners gesturing, with one fist clenched and one stiffened arm pointing beyond the horizon of the park. They shouted something, as hoarse as rooks, then their voices pitched higher into uproar. The people who had come for a nice afternoon in the gardens stood where they were and stared.

40

'They're having a political altercation,' said a man with his children. 'Where's their NCOs?'

There was a sound of something flat hitting something flat – say a wet cloth on a kitchen table. It was a slap on the face. Just for a moment the girls could see Frédé staggering and holding his jaw in his hand like toothache, with thick blood running through the fingers, but it wasn't Lise who'd hit him, she was still half up and half down, but nowhere near him any more. It was one of the FLs, and now they were all going down in twos and threes, rolling on the ground in squalor, with banging heads and seams splitting, showing a flash of whitish-grey pants.

'The soldiers!' Della cried. 'They're fighting! They can't do that!'

Those who were on their feet snatched up the rolls from the counter of the refreshment van and the summer air was streaked with missiles. The woman in the navy-blue beret was running away towards the Round Pond. Money fell from her bag onto the grass. The food she had prepared was trodden to a pulp and thrust and plastered into angry faces. There was nothing to laugh at, the sight of the homesick boys battering away at each other was like the naked spirit of hate itself.

The torn bread lay scattered everywhere. 'They're not English, you can't expect them to understand the shortages,' Vi thought. 'Thank God there's Lise.' She was making her way towards them, looking swollen and ugly.

'Where's Frédé?'

Two policemen were approaching in the distance, followed by five or six corporals, who had perhaps been absent without leave in the wine-bars of Kensington. The riot died down, the culprits began to explain themselves.

'He won't stay', Lise sobbed, 'he doesn't want me any more. They hit him. He wants to go back to Lyons.'

'We'll have to take her with us, Della. She can't go back to that convent place looking like that. She's distraught.'

But Della was going out dancing at the Lyceum. 'I've got to go and get into my black, but it isn't that that takes the

41

time, it's ringing up to see if anyone can lend me some pearls or a white collar. If you're going to wear black you have to have some little touches.'

Vi did not contest this. 'You can come home with me for a bit,' she said to Lise. 'My mother won't mind.'

They took a bus to Hammersmith. Vi paid both their fares, as although Lise had succeeded in hanging on to her bag she seemed, as often, to have no money with her. But it was a mercy she hadn't lost her BBC pass and identity card.

They walked up a quiet side road, simmering in the late afternoon heat.

The gate of Vi's home hung open among shaggy evergreens.

'Don't shut it, it's always open.'

'It's a big house,' said Lise.

'It has to be. There's nine of us.'

She went into the dark hall, lit by stained glass, with the air of an eldest child who expects to restore order, and listened for a moment to the noises from radios, hammers, pulled lavatory chains, taps running and a piano banging to identify who was at home, and whether they were more or less doing what they ought to be.

'You can't come across the hall, it's the English Channel', said a small boy who was sitting on the stairs.

'Where's Dad?'

'Still at the shop.'

'Where's Mum, then?'

She was thought to be putting on the kettle. To oblige the child they retreated through the front door and walked round by the lawn, dug up and planted with vegetables, the one rose-bed, the rabbit-hutches, coal-shed and coke-shed, and entered the kitchen by the back scullery.

'You want to put these in water at once, Mum,' said Vi, lifting a pile of crimson ramblers out of the sink. 'This is Lise Bernard, from work.'

Mrs Simmons was a broadly-based woman in an overall, not at all disconcerted by Lise's appearance. Having revived her memories of 1914, she in fact expected girls to be in tears. There was no question as to where Vi's kind heart came from. At home, however, one of her duties was to moderate its excesses.

'Sit down, Lizzie,' cried Mrs Simmons, who didn't get names right. 'You needn't mind showing your feelings. I daresay tea will help. But I can't pretend it'll alter the fact that he's far away.'

'He's in Kensington Gardens,' said Vi.

She kept remembering Frédé's face, dark and mad, with the blood oozing through his fingers.

'Perhaps Lise could share my room for a bit. She could manage ten shillings a week on what we get, couldn't you, Lise?'

In both Mrs Simmons' mind and Vi's the three-year-old's cot moved out of Vi's room and one of the boys went onto the lounge sofa and to compensate for this Chris, the merchant seaman, was asked to bring him something special by way of a souvenir. There was no need for either of them to explain further. It would be no trouble at all.

Lise appeared to be glad to leave the convent, but who could tell what she really thought? She seemed to have relapsed into her old sloth. One would say that she had given up the power of choice. Yet ten days later she left her job at Broadcasting House without saying goodbye. She did not come back to Hammersmith either, and Mrs Simmons couldn't think what to do with her few things. Finally Vi forbade her to mention the subject more than twice at any one suppertime.

3

'Jeff,' shouted Sam, 'do you remember that French general that came to the studio and died?'

'Yes.'

'Has anyone told you that you buggered up the whole thing?'

'Not in so many words.'

'But just tell me this, have you faced the fact that we didn't record him, not one single word? Nothing in the can, nothing to process for Archives. If you'd got to mess about with the transmission you could at least have put him on to closed circuit. Nobody bothered to tell me this, of course. It's only just been brought to my notice.' Jeff felt relieved. If Sam had indignantly offered to go to his defence, or even realized that some defence might be necessary, the situation would have been so disturbed that he'd have felt sea-sick. Nations fall, relationships have a duty to stay firm.

Sam's rage subsided into a regretful, eager anxiety. 'We've no decent French atmosphere, those Free French signing on were very disappointing, I've had Vogel in to listen to them and he just kept shaking his head. The wine coming out of the barrel isn't satisfactory.'

'We might try substituting white for red, perhaps.'

Sam ignored him.

'And now they say they're bringing Eddie Waterlow back from Drama to do some programme, *France Fights On* was the provisional title, sixty minutes of transcriptions I bloody well shouldn't wonder.'

'They're not exactly bringing him back, it's only that he wrote them such a very sad letter. He doesn't understand life in Manchester. He's never lived north of Regent's Park before. I don't suppose his programme will ever come to anything.'

'The point is that I oughtn't to be harassed about programme material at all – I oughtn't even to be consulted – the only thing that's of interest to me at the moment, the only thing I can think about and talk about, that is whenever I'm lucky enough to find anyone in this place who has the slightest comprehension of what I'm saying, the thing that's so much more important to me than happiness or health or sanity, is the improvement I'm hoping to make to the standard microphone windshield. The windshield, I mean, for the mobile units in battle areas. Whatever they choose to say, Directors, DG, Higher Command, War Cabinet, Prime Minister, you name it, I'm not sending my units back into Europe without a better windshield than the one they've got.'

'When do you envisage this new invasion taking place?' asked Jeff with interest.

'Not for six months. I'll have it ready by then. They'll have to wait till then.'

They had been on the telephone, but Jeff now went down to the third floor. Sam was sitting with a scale drawing in front of him. Mrs Milne was just leaving the room, and remarked: 'I've just been saying to RPD that by the end of the present emergency none of us will feel inclined to trust foreigners again.' But she could scarcely be heard above the deafening sound of *The Teddy Bears' Picnic* which was playing at high volume on one of the turntables. *Today's the day they're having the Teddy Bears' Picnic....* It was the engineers' favourite testing record, with its curious changes from low level to high. Jeff lifted the needle and switched off.

'Don't do that!' cried Sam.

'You know I'm not interested in your box of tricks.'

'I'm obliged, in the face of criticism, and my present state of under-manning, to do two things at once.'

'I think you ought to come out for a bit.'

'Out? Out?' Sam took off his glasses and gazed with his child's eyes.

45

His expression changed and he spoke humbly.

'Perhaps I don't lead a very healthy life. If ever I do go out of BH I hope I don't look different from other people, but I feel different.'

'Do you mean you're getting afraid to leave the place at all?'

'They don't seem to encourage me to go out with the cars any more. I don't know why that is.'

'I didn't mean that. I was thinking of your own place, Streatham Drive, isn't it, I came to dinner there last summer, perhaps you remember.'

'I'd like to ask you again, but I don't quite know if anyone's there.'

'Who knows if you don't?'

'My wife's evacuated herself, you know, to the country.'

'You haven't mentioned it.'

Sam pondered.

'She's learning to drive a tractor, which I rather think she's always wanted to do. A friend of hers is married to a farmer, they're producing Vegetables for Victory. Plums, too, I think, all this is near Pershore.'

'How many acres?'

'How many acres do people have? What are you talking about? You don't know anything about farming anyway. We were discussing the Archives. They're threadbare. It's not only omissions through mismanagement, like your general. For example, we've no Stukas. When we're asked for dive-bombing we have to borrow from Pathé Gazette.'

Jeff envied Sam the number of things he didn't notice, and even more his absorption in a fairy-tale world of frequency responses, a land of wire and wax where *The Teddy Bears' Picnic* was the password and the Fool could walk protected by his own spell. It was less envy, though, after all, than playing with envy, but it reminded him that when he himself had got out of the army and finished at Cambridge he had certainly not intended to be an administrator. Perhaps even now he could scarcely be called that, as his system depended so largely on considering his own comfort. Even his refusal to have a secretary was a kind of luxury, enabling him to ignore at least half his correspondence as not worth a reply. The Old Servants, though they had never been able to fault his methods, could not accept them. 'DPP will hardly be able to do without a secretary if tea-rationing is introduced,' Mrs Milne had begun to say, 'and it's threatened.'

On the 20th June Jack Barnett of Transport, Supply and Equipment asked if DPP could spare him a few minutes.

'Mr Haggard, do you still want that taxi to wait for you every night in Riding House Street?'

'Why, is the driver objecting?' asked Jeff. 'I should have thought he might have come and talked to me himself. He often does.'

'Not as far as I know. Of course, you're paying for his time yourself so he doesn't come onto my account. But I was thinking that perhaps you're not aware that since the news got so bad you're entitled as a Departmental Director to the use of an armoured car every evening on standby until further notice. Of course we're leaving it to your public spirit to share the car whenever possible.'

'Jack, you want my taxi for somebody else. Who is it?'

'Well, we've been notified that a very distinguished American newscaster is going to turn up here. He's just made his own way out of France, and NBS have asked us to give him transport facilities. We don't know how long he'll be over here, but he's said to be one of Britain's firmest friends, and believe me, Mr Haggard, we need them now.'

'He can have my armoured car.'

'I'm afraid I haven't made my point clear, Mr Haggard. He wants a cab with a Cockney driver who's a bit of a character. That's what journalists like, and that's what he is, newscaster's just their word for it. And you seem to be the only member of staff that can get a cab to wait regularly.'

'What's he called?'

47

'Something McVitie.'

DPP looked somewhat moved, you could almost call it pleased, but all he said was: 'If it's Mac, it will do him good to walk.'

The door seemed to explode inwards. It was fortunate that the desk was always kept clear, because the man who came in immediately piled it high with tin hats, webbing belts, mess-tins, three cameras, a Press arm-band, a bedroll, French wines, French cheeses, a holster, a .45 automatic and a pair of officer's field-glasses.

'Take all this junk out of here,' said Jeff.

Mac flung down a large sack of oranges and threw his arms round Jeff, as when brave and reluctantly friendly paleface meet. Barnett was taken aback. He'd never seen anybody, man, woman or child, attempt to embrace DPP and he could hardly credit it now.

'These are times of stress, times of decision,' growled Mac in a deeply rich New Jersey accent. 'I find you sitting here.'

'That's all I'm required to do until the Germans cross the Channel,' Jeff replied. 'I expect to get further instructions then.'

'Let's go on a real beat-up,' said Mac. 'You too, kid,' he added, turning to Barnett.

Barnett excused himself. His duties in regard to the important American correspondent were at an end. DPP and he were evidently as thick as thieves and could decide for themselves about the taxi. Meanwhile it was time to address himself to his next problem. The newly-installed French section didn't like the grade 3 mid-green carpets which he'd supplied with such difficulty. It was a moral issue, it seemed, they wanted to bivouac in the simplest possible conditions and to purify themselves through suffering, London being their new front line until victory was in sight. Now he was left with three carpets on his hands.

Up till 1939 Mac had been stationed in London rather more often than in other parts of the world, and on routine visits to BH he had got to know Jeff as well perhaps as anybody did. He loved Jeff because he saw him as a human being not over-impressed by the world, less so in fact than anyone he knew except his own grandmother who'd always refused to leave Stony Ridge, Vermont. Hence when Jeff had had to go to New York on the BBC's business or his own, he had always stayed with the McVitie family, out on Long Island.

Now Mac's unexpected arrival and generous progress through Broadcasting House was like a gust of warm wild air, exposing its thin places. At his approach Barnett had become a kid, while the office, ready for a forward planning meeting, had turned into a dump for left luggage. Even the well-tried national defence of expecting the worst, in which Jeff shared because it suited him temperamentally, had to give way and let through the impatient pioneer. Everything seemed possible, except to leave things as they were.

The two of them crossed the road together in the sunlight for a drink at the Langham. The vast hotel, rented by the BBC, gave the impression of being too proud to submit to its new occupants. The cathedral-like apse, the colossal Corinthian pillars branching into gilded foliage, the antique iron fire escapes, the pendants of Lalique glass glimmering from the high ceilings, all suggested many cycles of art and civilization, now put to baser uses and menaced by war. Upstairs, most of the bedrooms had been converted with hardboard partitions into offices; turning left through the mighty glass doors you came to a bar which the BBC had furnished with timid cocktail stools.

Mac drove his way through the clearings between the tables.

'My cut-through to New York's at seven. We've got half an hour. Do they have anything to drink here?'

'Give them time,' said Jeff. 'When you come into the war they'll lay in some root beer for you.'

'What do you want me to fight your war for?' Mac asked. He took a bottle of bourbon out of his coat pocket and offered the barman a drink in exchange for the loan of two clean glasses. 'What's the idea, why are you so anxious to survive?'

'Habit,' said Jeff.

'You ought to think about it very carefully. You'd get to be sixty or seventy, and then what are you going to do with yourself?'

'I shall care about less things.'

'As it happens my father's sixty-three to-day,' Mac went on. That makes me feel pretty young. Who was that character anyway, that one who was talking with you and couldn't come out? I'd hoped to ply him with liquor, I'd imagined he'd be the better for being plied.'

'He was consulting me about a taxi, but I rather think he was going on to the question of carpets.'

For the first time Mac's creased affectionate face was completely serious.

'You take on the hell of a lot too much of this advice and assistance. You're weakening these people. In times like these we've got to forgo luxuries and that includes the obligation to help others. Probably you ought to be doing something totally else.'

Over the different accents and languages at almost every table of the Langham Mac's lazily purring voice could be distinctly heard.

'Anyway, I'm told you've been in trouble.'

Jeff was not disconcerted, he didn't mind when heads turned round to look at him from a wide circle of tables, but he was surprised.

'When did you hear that?'

Mac, pouring out more bourbon, said that he's been to see all his contacts as soon as he landed. He'd come over just before dawn in a Breton fishing boat.

'Breton fishermen at dawn are the equivalent of Cockney taxi-drivers,' said Jeff. 'You'll choke yourself on local colour.'

'Let's get this right, I was told you'd been in trouble,' Mac persisted. 'Nobody said you were now. But a trouble-making capacity is God's gift, Jeff. You'll have to render an account some day of what the hell you did with it and the quality of the trouble you made. Don't tell me you're giving up just when you're getting your hand in.'

Jeff looked at him meditatively. 'Do you mean to say you went round all your contacts with that load of cheeses?'

'No, I dropped off quite a few of them as I went by. They were gifts.'

'What about all that stuff in my office?'

'Gifts, gifts. That's one of the things that's wrong with you, Jeff. You don't recognize a giver.'

Mac's call to New York came through on time and an hour later he flew home, either to get a clean shirt or to find a shirt that would fit him, there were two versions. He said he'd be back in September. That would be about the right time, according to his sources. Before leaving he had scattered oranges, which were unobtainable in England, and it wasn't clear where he could have got them in France, throughout the offices of BH. The strange fruit glowed from the bottom of in-trays and out-trays; a dozen of them were rolling about the deserted music library. The Recorded Programmes Assistants received three between the four of them who were left – Tad had gone to train as a fitter with the Free Polish Air Force. Willie and Vi waited until two minutes to fourteen hours, when Teddy and the yawning Della turned up on shift, while they were due to go off. The division of the oranges was a serious matter, since the shortages had produced in the whole population a delicate and bizarre sense of justice. The only sharp knives were in Packing and Despatch – the canteen had none – and Willie undertook to get hold of one.

They laid the three oranges on a copy of the *Radio Times*. It is difficult to know what to do with scarce items in wartime and David was no doubt right, when his servants risked their lives to bring him water, to pour it out on the ground as an offering to the Lord. For the RPAs, it came to three-quarters of an orange each. They were, of course, much too old to be greedy. Vi made a sensible calculation that it wouldn't be worth taking hers home to share it with so many. Willie picked up the packers' knife.

'Ten seconds from now.'

'Poor old Tad, I miss him,' said Teddy. 'I'd like to send him his slice.' None of them mentioned Lise.

'How are you going to work it out?' asked Della. 'One of them's smaller than the others.'

'That's a point.'

'. . . Aah, the Three Oranges . . . I am the Magician Tehelio . . .' sang a thin, disturbing tenor from the corridor. A lean and silvery figure sidled past.

'It's Mr Waterlow,' said Vi. 'He was down here before, when I first came, in January.' Surely he couldn't want a piece?

'I believe there's plenty of oranges in the other departments, Mr Waterlow,' snapped Della. But of course, he scarcely belonged to a department. He'd drifted back to London to do Heaven knows what.

'Ah, my dear, I have never brought myself to touch one . . .' he drifted on, and they could hear him start singing again, further down the passage.

Willie drew the sharp edge of the blade across the brilliant, delicately pitted skin of the first orange, and let it slide through the pith. Like a firework it sprayed up and burst into fragrance. The best moment. They sat licking and lingering, wondering if it was worth planting the pips, the heating would be on in BH next winter, but they wouldn't thrive, plants always knew the difference.

Della finished some time after the others. She was reading a General Circulation memo headed Christmas Arrangements 1940. The BBC, like most British organizations, thought about these in June. It began *Although it is not possible to forecast what shape this year's Christmas Programmes will take, or to give any assurance as to whether His Majesty will broadcast to the nation as he did in 1939, all Departments are asked to send in their*

52

suggestions as soon as possible. The Corporation also feels that it is not too early to warn staff, particularly in the Drama and Variety Departments, that all presents offered to them by the outside public, particularly money, jewellery, and alcoholic drinks, should be refused or returned as soon as possible, without comment.

'I'm going to apply for a transfer,' said Della.

They stared at her, with the limp empty quarters of peel in their hands.

'If Eddie Waterlow can come down from Drama, I don't see why I shouldn't go up there. It's a free country.'

'Jewellery!' Teddy exclaimed.

'You know I've always wanted to do something with my singing. I can't get anyone to audition me here. I believe I'd meet with understanding in Drama.'

'Everyone understands you down here,' said Vi.

'I've had my voice described as dark brown velvet,' Della said.

Teddy jumped up, putting the peel in his pocket, and told her that they'd be late if they didn't look out.

Mrs Milne's confidential crony, the Secretary of Assistant Director (Establishment), spoke to her without reserve. AD(E) simply didn't think that RPD knew how to select his staff. That last RPA, the half-French girl who snivelled, had left without even handing in her BBC pass and had left no forwarding address. And now he'd lost another one, although of course Zagorski, T., couldn't be blamed for joining his country's armed forces.

'What do you suggest, then? We're very short-handed.'

'It might be a much better plan to try for a sensible middle-aged woman, I mean someone a few years older than ourselves. Of course the job and the pay are on a junior scale, but that mightn't matter if she was just augmenting her husband's income. It's been demonstrated time and again that older women are less prone to tears and hysteria. I could show you our reliability charts. There's no reason at all why they shouldn't handle the discs efficiently, and if it came, as I believe it does, to holding RPD's hand when he feels under the weather, then one would imagine that they'd have had considerably more practice.'

'That, I think, is rather a delicate area where RPD has been very much misunderstood,' replied Mrs Milne. 'RPD likes to chat quietly about day-to-day problems of the Department and its very unfortunate that my hours of work make it impossible for me to listen to him as often as in his heart of hearts he would like.'

The two women were simply aiding and abetting each other to disband the Seraglio. Mrs Milne had allowed herself to take another step forward into illusion, and her friend, also an Old Servant, had not dissuaded her. AD(E) had insisted that this time a small panel should interview the applicants for the job of RPA, to avoid any repetition of mistakes. Both secretaries would attend it, and Mrs Milne thought that if they could guarantee to get through the business quickly, DPP might be prevailed upon to come too. She knew that he was devoted to RPD's interests, in spite of his sour manner; well, if not sour, you could hardly call it encouraging. However, she personally believed that DPP's main function – although he did his own job exceedingly well, no-one denied that – was to encourage RPD and to help him over those moments of depression which come to even the best of us.

The question of Lise's replacement also weighed heavily on RPD himself. For Establishment to count her as one of the girls he'd used up was a characteristic injustice. He had put her on his Emergency List, and told Mrs Milne that she was a somewhat unusual person, and surely needed special consideration, but only in a half-hearted manner, and before he had got to know her at all, she had simply disappeared.

'You might, perhaps, consider someone who would stay a little longer,' said Jeff. AD(E) had privately told him in advance that he'd have to assist in conducting the interview this time and see that a sensible appointment was made or there'd be nothing doing.

'They claim that in the present situation all the girls are needed for Coastal Defence,' said Sam, 'but that's ludicrous. I see girls walking about everywhere.'

'Do you mean you've actually been out?'

Sam ignored this. He was hurt and puzzled. 'Jeff, they want to surround me with old women. You know, there's a good deal of sagging on the late night shift, just when hopefulness is needed, and firmness, and roundness, and readiness to be pleased, and so on.'

'Have you mentioned this to Mrs Milne?'

'What's she got to do with it? I couldn't carry on if I didn't know that she was going to leave every day at half past five. And you know I've always had the best possible relationships with the junior members of my Department. I consider myself as morally responsible for them all and I can honestly say that I know their troubles as well as I do my own.'

Jeff felt that that was saying a good deal. He waited silently.

'Then there's another thing, I'm not sure I've made myself absolutely clear about my wife. Leaving London was her idea, not mine. I don't want you to think she's in any way out of the picture, just because she's never here. She sent me a photograph of the tractor, quite a good one. She seems to be occupied with the War Agricultural Committee which gets rather in the way of things, and then they all have coffee in each others' houses for some reason, and she's in the Red Cross with some friends of hers, splendid women, she tells me. The truth is that other things being equal she really prefers women to men.'

'So do you, Sam,' said Jeff.

He arranged for a recruitment interview at the end of the following fortnight.

4

It was reassuring to see the interviews and provisional Christmas arrangements going ahead and looking as they always had done while Broadcasting House reached its final state of War Emergency. The defence rooms were shut off by iron doors, armed guards patrolled the sub-basement, and the lists of Indispensable Personnel, except for Sam's, were complete. After repeated consultations Sam still hesitated as to who might be asked to accompany him, perhaps for weeks on end, behind the barricades. Meanwhile all departments were asked to find volunteers for the Red Cross Certificate Course.

Accommodation put the now unused concert-hall at the disposal of the Red Cross classes. The canvas-seated chairs, drawn up too close together for comfort just beneath the platform, conjured up the rapt ghosts of the BBC's old invited audiences. The lighting, designed for the orchestras now stranded in Bristol, was not too well suited to the lecturer, a harassed doctor from the nearby Middlesex Hospital who had probably expected younger listeners. Some of them, it was true, didn't look much more than children, but among them were departmental heads and even an Assistant Controller with folded arms, unused to sitting on a chair without a conference table in front of him. All ranks had been mingled to learn elementary first-aid. The BBC had always been liable to these sudden appealing man-ifestations of the democratic spirit, derived from both its moral and its veteran-theatrical sides, reminding both highest and lowest that they shared the same calling and, at the moment, the same danger.

'In cases of emergency,' muttered the lecturer,' an umbrella, walking-cane or broomstick is sure to be handy, and will furnish an excellent splint.' Unashamedly reading out of a hand-book, he went on: 'When a fracture has taken place the object is to bring the ends of the broken bone as nearly as possible to the position they were in previous to the accident. In order to do this, the part nearest to the body must be steadied by someone, while that furthest removed is gently stretched out, the sound limb being uncovered and observed as a guide. . . . For God's sake, ladies and gentlemen, don't dream of doing any of these things. Leave the patient exactly as he is, and if you have to move him take him straight round to Casualties. However, my object, as I understand it, is to see that by the end of six weeks you can be passed competent in bandaging, simple and compound fractures, first and second degree burns, lesions, cramp, poisoning, intoxication, snakebite . . . no need to take all these down, they're simply some of the chapter headings. . . .'

As soon as he decently could the doctor passed on to practical work, asking them to envisage the scene after a general attack from the air, but to assume, for the sake of convenience, that all the casualties were broken bones. DPP, sitting at the extreme edge of a row to make room for his long legs, was summoned to the front to take the part of an incident. Unruffled and resigned, labelled Multiple Injuries and Compound Fractures, he was laid out prone on one of a long line of stores trolleys. While the other incidents settled themselves he passed the time by smoking a cigar, which is difficult when both arms are immobilized.

'Perhaps you'd like me to copy out my notes for you as I go along, Mr Haggard,' said Willie Sharpe, bent over him and prodding him with a pencil, 'you'll probably miss a number of important points while you're lying here.' He scribbled rapidly. 'I've got you down as both femurs, both collarbones and right patella.'

Jeff emitted a faint cloud of smoke. The lecturer glanced at him in understandable annoyance. The cause of realism wasn't served by a multiple fracture smoking a cigar.

'Please will the incidents remember not to make signs or convey information of any kind to the class.'

Willie, however, had understood that DPP wanted the ash tipped off his cigar. He did so, then, not wishing to waste an opportunity, he drew up a chair, sat down near the trolley, and leant forward eagerly, half confiding, half appealing.

'We mustn't grudge the time we're spending on this Red Cross course, Mr Haggard. In fact, personally speaking, I'm very glad of the training because it contributes in a small way to one of my general aims for all humanity. I mean the maintenance of health both in mind and body. Education will be a very different thing in the world of tomorrow. It will start at birth, or even earlier. It won't be a petty matter of School Certificate, the tedious calculations of facts and figures which hold many a keen and hopeful spirit back to-day. It will begin as we're beginning now, Mr Haggard, you and I and all these others here this evening, with a knowledge of our own bodies and how they can be kept fighting trim – fighting, I mean, needless to say, for the things of the spirit. Yes, we shall learn to read our bodies and minds like a book and know how best to control them. Oh boy, will the teachers be in for a shock. Don't think, either, that I'm saying that physical desires must be entirely subdued. On the contrary, Mr Haggard, they have their part to play if every individual is to develop his potentialities to the full. And the point I want to make is how very little pounds, shillings, and pence have to do with all this. Yes, sir, out in the fresh air and sunlight, with your chosen mate by your side, you'll have little need for money.'

Carried away, glowing and translated into a generous future, Willie tucked away his notebook and pencil and passed on to the next trolley. As soon as he decently could the doctor hurried away, leaving two of his hospital nurses to carry on. At half-time, incidents and students were asked to change places. Jeff was released, and Willie became a shock case.

*

The following week a message was posted on all notice boards for the attention of volunteers for Red Cross training. The classes had been amalgamated with other local courses, and they were asked to attend in future at Marylebone Town Hall. Accommodation, it turned out, needed the concert-hall for a dormitory. In the event of an attack, the notice explained, personnel would be unable to get home, shift workers found it difficult already, and it hadn't escaped Accommodation's notice that a number of the staff never seemed to leave the building at all. In this connection, it should be emphasized that the new bathrooms on the fifth floor were for the use of grades of Assistant Controller and above. But in future the Corporation would provide beds for those who had earned them, strictly allocated on a ticket basis.

Quantities of metal bunks were dragged into Broadcasting House. Piled outside the concert-hall, they made an obstruction on the grand scale. Even the news readers, whose names and voices were known to the whole nation, were held up on their way to the studios. Even John Haliburton, assigned to read in case of enemy landing, with a voice of such hoarse distinction that if the Germans took over BH and attempted to impersonate him the listeners could never be deceived for a moment – even the beloved Halibut fell over a consignment of iron frames and himself became an incident. But the work went on with the exalted remorselessness characteristic of anyone who starts moving furniture. The bunks were fitted on top of each other in unstable tiers, and the platform, including the half-sacred spot where the grand piano had once stood, was converted into cubicles. Eddie Waterlow, insanely fond of music, was seen walking away from the sight with his head in his hands, a pantomime of grief. The fitters didn't mind, feeling that he acknowledged the importance of their work. If Broadcasting House had been built like a ship, it now had quarters for a crew of hundreds.

At length a cord was stretched across the great hall, dividing it in half, and grey hospital blankets were draped over it in place of a curtain. Barnett and his staff thought this part of the job by no means up to standard.

'It'll provide privacy for the ladies, which is the main point. But I don't like to see a job left like that.'

And might not the makeshift nature of the blankets lead to moral confusion? There were a lot of very young people among the temporary staff. Barnett was asked whether he thought there'd be goings on?

'Surely not while England's in danger' he replied.

Everyone went to look at the arrangements. 'So near and yet so far,' Teddy said. At the end of the week the RPAs' tickets arrived with their time-sheets. They were relieved, all of them, to think they wouldn't have to queue any more for the all-night buses.

When Vi got home that afternoon a little brother, lying flat on his back on the lawn where the cabbage beds had become torpedoes, and he was drowned and floating, told her that someone had rung her up. When she went into the hall the telephone rang again.

'Vi, it's Lise.'

'Where are you? Are you coming back to work?'

'Vi, I want you to help me. I haven't anywhere to live.'

'Why don't you go home? Southampton's a defence zone, but of course it'll be all right for you if your parents live there.'

'I can't get on with them. I don't feel as though I'm their child at all. I don't want to hear what they say about Frédé. When my father starts up about Frédé I feel like doing him an injury.'

'Well, Lise, we're full up here at the moment, I'm sorry. I don't know whether . . .'

'Listen, it isn't for long, only for a night or so. I haven't any money, but I'm going to get a job, then I shall have money. Listen, Vi, is it true they've got places to sleep now in Broadcasting House?'

'Have you been back there, then?'

'No, I read it in the *Daily Mirror*.'

'Well, we get the *Mirror*, but I missed that.'

60

'It was headed THIS IS THE NINE O'CLOCK SNOOZE.'

'I didn't see it.'

'Vi, please get me a ticket, I've still got my pass, they'll recognize me at Reception and they'll never know I've left. It's only for a very short time.'

Vi considered. There was an extra ticket, it had been sent by mistake for Della, and should have been given back immediately to Mrs Milne. Of course, if Lise was found out it would be awkward, but on the whole it wasn't likely. They would think she'd been away in one of the regions, or on a training course, which heaven knows she'd needed badly enough.

'I can get you a ticket, Lise, but where shall I send it to?'

'Leave it at Reception in an envelope with my name on it. I'll pick it up. You needn't have anything more to do with it, you needn't see me or talk to me.'

Although she found the pathos of this last remark irritating, Vi was dissatisfied with herself. What she had been saying fell short of the truth. The house, by her family's standards, wasn't full up; the other bed in her room was free. But looking back over the last six weeks or so she thought of Lise in a state of doleful shapelessness, only half listening while her job was explained to her, then collapsing into tears it seemed, when RPD was doing no more than beginning to talk to her – and after all nobody in BH worked harder than he did – then the unpleasantness about Frédé and Lise's dampening presence in the house, Dismal Lizzie the little ones had called her and had to be threatened into silence, and finally even her mother having one or two things to say when she disappeared without explanation. Vi had been able to tell from one look at her mother's back, as she started the washing-up, that she was hurt. Surely that was justification enough for not having Lise back.

And then, she was expecting Chris on leave, pretty well certainly this time. 'I hope he keeps strong for you,' said Teddy gloomily, a spectator of experience, always on the wrong side of the windowpane. Sometimes he went down to the BH typing pool to see if any of the girls would like to come out, say to the pictures, or for a cup of tea at Lyons. Their heads, dark and fair, rose expectantly as he came in, then, although he was quite nice-looking, sank down again over their work. Nor was Teddy very popular with the Old Servant who supervised the pool.

The Department was getting a new girl as a replacement, but what use was that? He'd read an article by a psychologist in some magazine or other which explained rather well how owing to Nature's Law of Compensation girls in wartime, if they weren't fixed up already, were practically bound to fall in love with older men. That was a scientific analysis, and you couldn't fly in the face of science.

All the same, he allowed himself a mild interest in the newcomer. During his tea-break he went and hung about the second floor. The corridor, like all the others, curved mysteriously away, following the lines of the outer walls, and leading to sudden shipboard meetings, and even collisions, as the door opened. Most of Administration was there, and you could usually find out what was going on. While the tape machines in the basement ticked in the world's news from outside and radio gathered it from the air, the second floor generated the warm internal rumours of BH. There, through one of the filing clerks, a very plain girl, unfortunately, Teddy learned that they were considering an RPA application from Birmingham.

5

Annie Asra was the kind of girl to whom people give a job, even when they didn't originally intend to. Her name sounded foreign, but wasn't. She came from Birmingham.

Annie was a little square curly-headed creature, not a complainer. Certainly, at seventeen, she would never have complained about her childhood. She had spent the part of it which was most important to her on the move, trotting round beside her father, who was a piano tuner. In the city of a thousand trades, he had seen his own decline, but he still had quite enough work to live on. He was a widower, and it was felt in the other houses in their terrace that he wouldn't be able to manage, but he did.

It was a curious existence for a child. Winter was the height of the piano-tuning season, and she became inured at an early age to extreme temperatures. The pianos that were considered good enough to tune were in little-used front parlours and freezing parish rooms, sometimes in the church itself where on weekdays a tiny Vesuvius struggled with the frost's grip, its stovepipe soaring high into the aisle vaulting. She didn't have to go, the neighbours would have minded her, but that didn't suit Annie. She knew all their regulars, who her father would have to speak to and where he had to hang up his coat. The pianos stood expectantly, some with the yellowed teeth of old age, helpless, once their front top was unscrewed, awaiting the healer's art. There were two Bechsteins on their round, one belonging to a doctor, the other to a builder's merchant, but Mr Asra didn't prefer them to the others. To each according to their needs.

It often seemed a very long time before the actual tuning began. The ailing pianos had to be put in good order first, cracks wedged up, the groaning pedals eased with vaseline. Annie was allowed to strike every key in turn to see if any of them stuck. If so, a delicate shaving of wood had to be pared away. Sometimes the felts needed loosening, or even taken right off, to be damped and ironed in the kitchen or the church vestry. They smelled like wet sheep under the iron, and lying all together on the board they looked like green or red sheep. Then they had to be glued back onto the hammers, and Mr Asra never did anything either quickly or slowly.

When at last he took out his hammer and mutes, ready to tune, his daughter became quite still, like a small dog pointing. While he was laying the bearings in the two middle octaves she waited quietly, though not patiently, watching for him to get the three C's right, tightening the strings a little more than necessary and settling them back by striking the keys, standing, bending, tapping, moving his hammer gently to and fro round the wooden pins, working through the G's, the D's and the A's until he came to middle E. When middle E was set Annie left the spot where he had put her, the warmest place, close to the stove, and stood at his elbow, willing him to play the first trial chord. It was a recurrent excitement of her life, like opening a boiled egg, the charm being not its unexpectedness but its reliability. And Mr Asra struck the chord of C.

'But the E's sharp, dad,' she said.

That too was in order, she always said it. To please her, he lowered the E a little, and sounded the perfect chord, looking round at her, an unimpressive man in his shirtsleeves and waistcoat, able to share with her the satisfaction of the chord of C major. But he couldn't leave it like that, she knew. The E must be sharpened again, all the thirds must be a little bit sharp, all the fifths must be a little bit flat, or the piano would never come right. At this point he quite often gave her a boiled sweet from a paper bag in the pocket of his waistcoat.

When he reached the treble Mr Asra worked entirely by

ear. The treble for Annie was entering a region of silver or tin, the wind through the keyhole, walking with due care over the ice, sharpening gradually until the uttermost tones at the top of the keyboard. With the bass she felt more at ease. There was danger, in that if a string broke it couldn't be replaced and had to be spliced there and then, but the tuning itself was easier, the strings ran easily and willingly over the bridges, and their warm growl took her downwards into a region of dark fur-covered animals crowned with gold who offered their kindly protection to the sleepy traveller. Annie, in fact, when she was very young, often fell asleep during the bass, even though she loved it best. The torrent of chromatic scales which signified the final testing, and which the householders thought of as the tuner (who'd probably once hoped to be a concert performer) letting himself go at last, didn't interest either of them nearly so much.

While her father was putting away his things into the familiar leather bag, worn threadbare round the edges, they were often brought a cup of tea, with two lumps of sugar put ready in the saucer. The owner, coming hesitantly out of some other room, looked at their piano, with everything screwed back and in order, as if it was a demanding relative newly come out of hospital. 'The Queen of the Home,' Mr Asra called it, when a remark of this kind seemed necessary. Sometimes there was a vibration of distress, which Annie deeply felt. 'If you're going to give singing lessons, madam, you really ought to have it tuned to concert pitch. I could do that if you want, but it may mean replacing a few strings,' and the pale-coloured woman could be seen to shrink, anxiety adding to her embarrassment over handing him the right money.

Annie became self-contained, a serious tranquil believer in life and in the time ahead when she would know what was most important to her. She went to school with her brown curling hair in decent pigtails. Her aunt, her dead mother's eldest sister, came in from next door every day to do it for her. At the end of her first morning at Church

School, when the teacher told them to go out for their second play, she half got up and then sat down again quickly, feeling her head dragged painfully back by a cruel weight. Dick Dobbs, the boy sitting behind her, had tied her pigtails to the back of her chair, perhaps with her aunt's new ribbon, perhaps with string. She sat there perfectly still until the teacher, who had gone out to patrol the yard, came back and found her sitting stiff and serious as a little idol. 'Why didn't you tell me as soon as class was done?' she asked, relieved that there were no tears.

'I wouldn't give him that satisfaction.'

At the end of the Christmas term there was a letter-box in the corner of the classroom. It was made from a dustbin covered with red crepe paper; the handles sticking out each side spoiled the illusion to some extent, but the teacher put a cardboard robin on each. In the box the children posted cards to one another, bought at Woolworths, carefully inscribed the night before, and brought to school in their cases that morning in an atmosphere of jealous secrecy. Some got few or no cards. The teacher could do nothing about this, the box was opened at mid-morning and she was unable to get at it in time to redress the balance. Annie, however, had plenty. When she was eight years old she received a large snow scene covered with glitter, beautiful, and from the expensive box. The rest of the class gathered round to admire until she slowly put it away in her case.

'I put that in the box for you,' said Dick Dobbs.

'It's a pretty card.'

The teachers asked her why, at Christmas time, she couldn't say something more friendly.

'He's a dirty devil,' Annie replied calmly. She accepted that people couldn't be otherwise than they were, good, bad, and middling, but one ought to be allowed to take them or leave them.

She kept seeing Dick, because although he didn't come on to grammar school with her friends, he sang in the same church choir as she did, at St Martin's. When she was twelve and a half he caught her behind the vicarage bicycle sheds, took a firm grip of her and pressed her back hard against the wall.

'I expect you think it's wrong to do this,' he said, unbuttoning her coat.

'I don't think it's wrong,' Annie replied. 'I daresay I'd do it if I liked it.'

He was disconcerted, hesitated and lost hold. Annie walked away, but not in a hurry, she stopped to do up the six buttons of her coat. There were one or two boys she liked at school, but not Dick. She'd not do any better for Dick by pretending. Luckily his voice was breaking.

Annie did well at her lessons, and would have liked to please the music teacher, who wanted her to start piano, but for reasons that were not clear to her, and therefore caused her annoyance, she didn't care to learn. Her father could have found the money, but he never made her do anything she didn't want to.

When she was nearly sixteen, Mr Asra fell ill. He asked Annie to make the round of the customers and tell them that unfortunately he wouldn't be coming. When she rang the bell-pulls which she hadn't been able to reach as a little girl, and saw through the front windows the familiar pianos, and the silver-framed photos on them that had to be moved away when the tuner called, she knew for certain that her father was going to die. The doctor couldn't make out what was wrong, but that was no surprise to their neighbours in the terrace, who were well aware that doctors don't know everything. Mr Asra didn't have to be sent away to hospital to die. Annie managed pretty well, sleeping on two chairs in the passage outside his room. He was with them one night and gone in the morning, when she got up to fetch him the medicine which the district nurse had left.

Her aunt, who lived next door, asked her to move in for the time being, and no-one could fault the arrangements. But they were not surprised, either, when in spite of the emergency Annie went off to try her luck in London. That was on the 8th of July, the day they announced the tea-rationing, two ounces per person per week.

Annie left her luggage and umbrella at Paddington and took the Underground, hoping, as the result of this, that she'd never have to travel in it again. The windows of the trains, following regulations, were painted black, with a tiny square of glass left to peer through and to make out the name of the station. This presumably meant that the tube came above ground some time, but it didn't do so before she got out at Oxford Circus.

The passers-by were quick to tell her that she couldn't miss Broadcasting House, because it looked like a ship with the wrong sort of windows. She walked right and left between the sandbags that masked the entrance and realized, from the way the sentry looked at her, that she'd done right to put on her white blouse and navy blue skirt.

The entrance hall of BH worried her not at all. It reminded her of the Midland Hotel, where once or twice, when a friend had been taken ill, her father had been called in to tune the concert grand. In its size and height she recognized the need to impress. People had to feel they'd arrived somewhere. She remembered, too, that they hadn't much wanted a child running around the hotel, so they'd told her to go and look at some comics in a little room upstairs, much like the room where she went for her interview now.

There were two middle-aged women who identified themselves as Mrs Milne and Mrs Staples, from Establishment. They were in charge, and yet she felt they needed approval from the man sitting rather apart from them, at the corner of the table, who wasn't much like anyone Annie had ever met. He was both pale and dark, and had the sort of face that they used to say would make a fortune on the halls; perhaps, indeed, he had. At the moment he was half lying back and looking at the ceiling, which made Annie wonder why he had come to interview her at all. It must be an advantage, she thought, to be like that, and not to bother.

'You don't need to be musical,' Mrs Milne explained, 'or to have any kind of technical knowledge – just complete accuracy in following instructions, punctuality and reliability. We've got the references from your Vicar and your head teacher . . . and then you've had a Saturday job as well, haven't you?'

'At Anstruthers,' said Annie. 'I was in the loose count sweets to start with, then they moved me to hosiery. We'd instructions to let the old folks help themselves to a few sweets if they wanted to,' she added.

'Their letter was satisfactory too,' murmured Mrs Staples.

'The job is largely chasing the recordings and seeing that they're available at the right time, and for the right programmes.'

'A straightforward service job,' said Mrs Staples.

Mrs Milne changed colour a little.

'Service, yes, but of a particularly important nature. The Department is quite indispensable to the Corporation as a whole. The name of your Director, by the way, if you were selected for this position, would be Mr Seymour Brooks. But you would be working on shift – you'll have to take that into account, by the way, when you're finding somewhere to live – and you're not likely to have much direct contact with Mr Brooks.'

Annie didn't miss the change from *you would* to *you will*, and she observed with compassion that Mrs Milne looked downright tired. Probably she'd been interviewing for hours and there'd been very few hopefuls.

Meanwhile the man stretched his legs and shifted in his chair as though he was thinking of going, causing an equal but contrary movement in the two women. Then he said, in a voice almost too quiet to catch: 'My name is Jeffrey Haggard. I have nothing to do, really, with your appointment, I'm the Director of Progamme Planning . . . You're from Birmingham, Miss Asra?'

They'd all said that, seeming to think it was rather surprising for her to come. However far away did they think it was?

'I've been through it often enough, but I've never stopped there. Tell me, just as a point of geographical interest, would you call Birmingham north or south?'

He smiled, and for the first time since she'd passed the soldier at the door, Annie smiled back.

'It's neither.'

'I imagine that perhaps there's only one way to settle it. Are there pork butchers, separate from the ordinary butchers?'

'Of course there are, Mr Haggard.'

'Then it must be north.'

Annie was wrong in thinking that there hadn't been many hopefuls among the applicants. There had been none at all. She had been right, however, in detecting, as she did, that her interviewers were not quite of one mind. Mrs Milne was thinking of RPD, Mrs Staples was thinking of AD(E), and Jeff wanted to get away.

'I think we might as well appoint her at once,' Mrs Milne said, straightening her back, when she was left alone with her friend. 'Of course, she'll have to go through the college, but I hardly anticipate. . . .'

By this she meant that the BBC would have to ascertain that Annie had never been a member of the Communist Party. But, in view of the understaffing in Recorded Programmes, they thought it safe to issue her with a temporary pass, and tell her to report for work on Monday.

The next problem, of course, was where the girl was to live. It was no use leaving things to chance, she might slip back to Birmingham. Mrs Milne had hostels in mind, but Vi, with Lise still on her conscience, went with Annie to Paddington to pick up the luggage and then brought her back to Hammersmith on that very first evening. Mrs Simmons, who was generous enough to learn nothing from

70

experience, welcomed a new lodger. She was bottling plums, and not ever remembering a year like it for plums. Hitler had given out that Britain would capitulate by August, she added, or rather he'd said it some time ago, but she'd only just read it off an old *Mirror* that she'd used to spread under the jars.

'Did you share a room before?' Vi asked, taking Annie upstairs.

'Not really, because I hadn't brothers and sisters.'

'Do children worry you, then?'

Annie shook her head.

'My little brothers don't need much,' Vi went on. 'Just fall down when they machine-gun you, half-way will do if we're at table.'

'I can manage that.'

'Well, I'll show you where to put your things. You'll have to make do with just a bit of the cupboard, because we've got all our winter things in there, and these two and a half drawers over here. How will that do?'

And after all, Annie had not brought much.

'What my mother meant, starting off about Hitler, and the jars, and everything, was that if there's any trouble you'd be better off in a house like this, where there's a lot of us.' She sat down on her own bed. 'Do you want to use the phone? Will they be worrying about you at home?'

'Writing will do,' said Annie stiffly. 'I don't think my aunt will be at her house. I think she's going to let it.'

Vi perceived that they had come to the end of that subject.

6

RPD had hit a snag in his design for lightweight recording equipment with an adequate – that was all he asked, heaven knew, that it should simply be adequate – windshield. At the moment he paid attention to nothing else, and nobody except the engineers had access.

'You'll have to await your summons,' said Teddy, sitting back, world weary, surveying Annie. 'That's what you have to expect in a Seraglio.'

Annie was annoyed at herself at first for not knowing what the word meant. She'd thought it was a kind of opera.

The first job she was called upon to undertake by herself was to check the whole series of de Gaulle's speeches, mark them up, and take them to the studio for the run-through of Eddie Waterlow's dramatic feature *France Fights On*. The programme had been scheduled some time ago and had changed its name several times during the German advance. Director (Home) thought that as the cast had been booked and a certain amount of money spent already, the whole thing had better be recorded before something happened to make further alterations necessary. Annie was afraid when she first got through the door with her armful of discs, because no-one was there but Mr Waterlow, dancing quietly round the restricted space in the control studio. They'd told her that there were Old Servants in Broadcasting House, but not that there were mad Old Servants. It was the Hesitation Waltz he was doing. He paused and looked at her searchingly.

'You've come early.'

'I wanted to make sure that everything was all right, Mr Waterlow.'

He asked her name, then remarked: 'I don't think I've seen you before. You are my Recorded Programmes Assistant for this afternoon?'

'Yes, Mr Waterlow.'

'When did you join the Corporation?'

'Last Monday, Mr Waterlow.'

'You appear bewildered.'

'Well, Mr Waterlow, it's my first time on duty.'

He peered at her. 'I don't know if you're addressing me in this respectful way as a jest.'

'They told me upstairs that was your name.'

'It is. I have no intention of asking you what else they said. I may be too sensitive. I fancied that after only a few days you had joined the conspiracy against me.'

He'd stopped dancing, except for a few steps forward and back.

'I'm not surprised in the least that the most inexperienced Recorded Programmes Assistant in the building has been assigned to me. If my abilities were ever highly valued by the Corporation, they are certainly not so now. Nevertheless I've been put in charge of a not unimportant programme, a tribute to the country without which Europe could hardly be termed civilised. And yet, in asking me to do this, they may have asked too much. Somewhere along the way I've lost the one quality necessary to preserve the glitter and the illusion, not only of the theatre – even in wartime I put that first – but of life. I mean confidence. All mine is gone. And from your expression at the moment, I fear you have none either.'

'I've got plenty of confidence, Mr Waterlow,' said Annie. 'It's just that you talk so daft.'

She put her records neatly in the producer's rack. You couldn't help liking him. Exhausted by his tirade, he watched her dreamily.

'I think you must come from Birmingham. . . . What made you come to Broadcasting House?'

'I wanted to do my bit.'

'Ah, you can stand there and say that! I couldn't say it without the deepest embarrassment. The deepest! I envy you.'

A Junior Programme Engineer stuck his head round the door, saw Annie, and whistled.

'Got the running order, sweetheart?'

'Yes, it's announcement, narrator one minute twelve, cross-fade Marseillaise thirty seconds, fade out. . . .'

'Yep, that's what I came to tell you, Eddie,' said the JPE casually, 'European wanted me to remind you. You can't fade the Marseillaise, not for the duration, to avoid offence to our Allies.'

Mr Waterlow sank down in picturesque despair. 'My timing. . . .'

'Yep, the whole two minutes of it. All or nothing. You'll have to substitute.'

'Heartless, heartless children. . . .'

'Don't give way, Mr Waterlow,' Annie cried, 'It'll not take me a minute to go up to the Gram Library and get you a commercial. They showed me where it was on my tour of the building.'

'A spark. . . .'

'But what would you like me to get?'

'Anything . . .' His voice strengthened a little. 'Anything but the song-cycles of Hugo Wolf. The Gramophone Library seem to have an unending supply of them, just as the canteen never runs out of digestive biscuits . . . my dear, fetch me something that is not by Hugo Wolf . . . let it at least be French.'

When Annie returned with a commercial of *Ma Normandie*, which she'd been told could be faded out anywhere, the situation in the studio had changed. The JPE had left, but someone else had come, a little old man, not looking at all well, but with a fierce air of not letting himself go, and of having dressed for the occasion. He had on a yellow checked waistcoat and a blue suit, the trousers pressed like blades.

'Who are you? Who? Who?' cried Eddie Waterlow.

'The agent told me what time to come along.'

'Why? At whose prompting? Did they tell you that, regardless of what rehearsals may have been called and what confirmations may have been sent by Bookings, anyone and everyone is welcome at Eddie Waterlow's productions?'

'I've got my letter from Bookings,' said the old man. 'I'll take a chair if I may.'

He sat down with difficulty. 'I'm a bit stiff, you might say I've one leg and a swinger. I don't do much dancing nowadays.'

Annie wondered if she oughtn't to fetch him something. He looked bad; in fact, they both did.

'I've got my cast list here,' said Eddie, trying to maintain authority.

'What is your name?'

'Fred Shotto.'

'I have that on my list, certainly, but there must be a mistake of some kind. *Spotlight* gives him as twenty-nine years old, Shakespeare and classic comedy, specialises in French accent.'

'That'll be my son,' said the old man. 'He's with the forces now. He's Fred Shotto, junior. You can bill me as the old block he's a chip of.'

Encouraged by Eddie's silence, he went on: 'The booking was in my name, all right. You can't contest that, it's legal. I'm all right myself once I've got my confidence.'

He took out a roll of sheet music.

'I've brought my material.'

Eddie had chosen to sink his face into his left hand, while his right arm hung down helplessly towards the ground. Annie, feeling that someone must, took the music, from which other pieces of paper covered with writing fluttered to the ground.

'*That's* my material. The other's my opening number.'

'Annie! What has he brought me!'

Annie smoothed it out.

'It's the *I've Got The You Don't Know The Half Of It, Dearie Blues*, Mr Waterlow.'

The JPE thrust forcefully in again, this time winking broadly.

'How's it coming, curly? We're going to record in ten minutes.'

Annie went to the door.

'Mr Waterlow seems to be in difficulties. Do you think he's all right?'

'Live in hopes.'

But *France Fights On* was cancelled, shelved to make room for the mounting defence instructions. Perhaps, indeed, it had never been planned for; only DPP was likely to be able to give an answer to that.

Eddie Waterlow had considerable difficulty in getting rid of Fred Shotto. The old man, who had started out as a clog-dancer at the age of four, had learned persistence in a harder school, as he pointed out, than Hitler's war, and beyond that he had some idea that by getting work he was keeping the place warm for his son. Long after the cast had been dismissed he clung to his chair, and Eddie was obliged in the end to make a recording of the *I've Got The You Don't Know The Half Of It, Dearie Blues*, cracked and trembling, which might have become a collector's piece if it had not been consigned at once to scrap. Dislodged at last, and given a farewell drink, Fred Shotto became affectionate in the theatre's old way, telling everyone in sight that Mr Waterlow had made him a happy man, and advising them to lean on Jesus till the clouds rolled by. It turned out that he'd done some hard years, too, as a revivalist.

After his programme was lost, Eddie drifted round the building, assisting a little here and there, a pensioner of the arts such as Broadcasting House, even in wartime, could not bring itself to discourage. He was told that *France Fights On* 'might have involved falsification'; the BBC remained loyal to the truth, even when they stretched it a little to spare the feelings of their employees.

As an institution that could not tell a lie, they were unique in the contrivances of gods and men since the Oracle of Delphi. As office managers, they were no more than adequate, but now, as autumn approached, with the exiles crowded awkwardly into their new sections, they were broadcasting in the strictest sense of the word, scattering human voices into the darkness of Europe, in the certainty that more than half must be lost, some for the rook, some for the crow, for the sake of a few that made their mark. And everyone who worked there, bitterly complaining about the short-sightedness of their colleagues, the vanity of the news readers, the remoteness of the Controllers and the restrictive nature of the canteen's one teaspoon, felt a certain pride which they had no way to express, either then or since.

7

Sam Brooks asked Mrs Milne whether she'd noticed that there was a new Recorded Programmes Assistant.

'Perhaps one ought to keep a check on these things,' he said.

'She was interviewed by myself and a representative of Establishment,' replied Mrs Milne. 'DPP was also present.'

'Whatever for?'

'Her name is Annie Asra – I suppose Anne, I have put her on the register as Anne.'

'I don't quite see why I wasn't consulted. But I must have a word with her as soon as I can.'

Annie settled in easily with the Simmons. She gave no feeling of upset, rather of solidity and peace. Vi loved her mother, but was too much like her not to get irritated after fifteen minutes. She lent a hand whenever she was at home, but in her own way. To Annie, who had been reared by her widowed father, and brought to her present excellent state of health entirely on fish and chips and tins, there was a charm in helping Mrs Simmons around the garden and kitchen. It was unpatriotic now not to sort the rubbish into pigfood, henfood, tinfoil (out of which, it seemed, battleships could be partly made), paper, cardboard and rags. At the same time Mr Simmons worked late at the shop, sorting the coupons from the customers' ration books. The nation defended itself by counting large numbers of small things into separate containers. But beyond this there were the old repetitive tasks of the seasons, the parts which, in the end, seem greater than the whole. Annie sat on the back doorstep and shelled peas with Mrs Simmons. She had never done it before.

'You've only just come, and yet you're the only one in this house that does it with a sense of what's fair,' said Mrs Simmons. 'The others just take all the ones with the large peas in and then go away and leave me with the awkward ones.'

The pods were almost autumnal, and striped with paler colour. The hard late peas fell with a light percussion into the colander, then, as the pile covered the bottom, the sound changed to a rustle.

'I still think that's an unusual name, Asra,' Mrs Simmons went on. 'Vi's mentioned to me not to ask you about it, but if I always did whatever she tells me I'd never know anything. Is it Jewish, or Spanish, or what?'

'I don't think it's either,' Annie replied, 'but I don't mind your asking.'

'Well, I suppose you get all sorts of names in a big manu-facturing place. Perhaps it's taken out of the Bible.'

'My last head teacher told me it was the name of a tribe,' said Annie. 'I thought that was going a bit far.'

'Well, you'll change it one day. If you're a girl, you've always got that to look forward to.'

Vi had told her not to say that kind of thing, either. They sat there together calmly, their minds full of the July garden. After the peas, they'd have to do something about the runners.

'Look, there's seven peas in this one,' said Annie.

They both felt unreasonably happy. It wasn't much longer than any of the other pods, and yet none of them had had more than five.

Vi had come home, looking tired out.

'They'll be too hard to eat even when they're cooked,' she said, but not unkindly, looking at the whitish green heap.

'Well, these are the last we'll do this year.'

Annie got up, shook the bits of leaf and tendril off her lap into the pig bucket, and took the colander into the kitchen.

'She'll want to find something a bit more entertaining than sitting here helping me,' said Mrs Simmons, who always felt strangely impelled to talk about anyone who had just gone

79

away. 'You could take her to the Palais one evening when you're both off work together. The management's bought more than a thousand pairs of shoes, you know, so that the service-men can change out of their boots.'

'Well, I'll think about it when Chris gets back. But Annie's all right, Mum, she's only been at BH a week and there's plenty of boys would like to take her out. Teddy would, to start with.'

'Isn't that the one who talked to me so interestingly about the world to come?'

Mrs Simmons didn't know why it was that when Vi was at home and she particularly wanted to demonstrate her intelligence and power of memory, they both had to desert her at once. Of course, she'd confused Teddy with Willie Sharpe, who'd looked so young when he came to tea that she'd felt he ought to be out playing round the cabbage beds. But there was no need, really, for her daughter to correct her. All she needed was a little time to think.

On her second Monday, when Annie was passing RPD's office on her way to filing, the door opened and he looked out and shouted: 'Come in here!'

She knew him already, of course, by sight, but had no-one much to compare him with as an employer except the head buyer at Anstruthers, and that was not much help. The buyer had always been peaked with worry, whereas even at a distance from RPD she felt herself on the edge of a crazy enthusiasm, like a ring of magic fire; he looked to be as wrapped up in what he was doing as Vi's little brothers. As she went in and shut the door he retreated backwards and snatched up a new recording.

'Spirit of the Earth, come to my call,' he read from the handwritten label.

'Do you want me, Mr Brooks?' enquired Annie.

'They made this in Bristol yesterday and sent it up to me on the van. It's got nothing to do with any of our programmes here, it's music, baritone and orchestra, but they wanted me to hear it at once.'

'I don't know the song, I'm afraid.'

He looked at her impatiently. 'It doesn't matter what you know! I only want someone with two ears.' The waste of even a moment was unbearable.

'Sit down, sit down, for God's sake.'

He checked the pickup of his turntable and put on the record. Annie sat with her hands in her lap and listened, as he did, without shifting or stirring while the record played through twice.

'Well? Well?' shouted Sam.

'I liked the song, as far as that goes.'

'The song! What do I care if you liked it or not? I called you in here because you were the first person I caught sight of in the corridor and I wanted you to share my experience. Nothing is an experience unless it's shared. When I've got something in my hands that's as near perfection as we can hope for in wartime conditions my first reaction is, someone else must have the chance to listen to this. I oughtn't to have played it at all before it was dubbed. I know that. If my RPEs were here they'd want to grind me into powder. Above all I shouldn't have played it back to you twice as I did just now. But I wanted you to know once and for all what's meant by the term "quality" and the term "balance", and on top of that, there was the singer.'

'I'm very glad to learn about quality and balance,' said Annie quietly, 'but the singer was flat.'

'I don't understand you.'

'His first phrase he started out with was C E flat B flat D. He was in tune till the D, then he was a twelfth of a tone flat and didn't get back till his last bar but one.'

'Do you claim to be particularly musical?' Sam asked with dangerous calm.

'No, they asked me that at my interview, and I told them not.'

Sam began to pace about.

'Perhaps I should explain that while the performance and the recording are of course two different and independent things, my whole training and working life

81

suggest that I might fairly be considered as a judge of both. What's more, at this interview of yours, about which I was given no prior information, by the way, they may have made it clear to you – if not, indeed, you may realise it for yourself when you've been here rather longer – that I'm in charge of a department of which you too have become a part . . . feel that, please feel that and think about it . . . and in order to be sure that the strain doesn't become unendurable I have to look for a good deal of co-operation and human understanding and delicacy from my staff, all things that come naturally, I'm glad to say, to girls of your age.'

He took off his spectacles, and Annie met his defenceless gaze.

'It was flat, Mr Brooks.'

RPD asked Mrs Milne whether she'd noticed that the new RPA girl seemed rather different from anyone they'd ever had in the Department before.

'She does exactly the same hours as the others, Mr Brooks, and so far I've heard nothing to suggest that she's overworked, or that she doesn't get enough to eat, or that she needs any special consideration. She's fixed herself up with Violet Simmons' family, she's got a room in their house in Hammersmith. And if you're going to ask me whether she looks like some picture or portrait you've seen somewhere, I might as well tell you, in order to save time, that in my opinion she's a very usual-looking girl from the Midlands.'

Sam glanced up at his secretary in mild surprise.

'As it happens, her face does remind me of a portrait, but I can't quite place it. It might be Shelley. Did he have curly hair?'

'Everyone had curly hair in those days,' said Mrs Milne. 'It was the Spirit of the Age.'

'Where's the Picture Reference Library these days?'

'It was evacuated in the first week of the war, Mr Brooks.'

She waited for further instructions, but Sam said: 'I don't want that girl on my Indispensable Personnel List.'

The list by this time had worked itself down to the middle of the Defence Instructions file. Mrs Milne concealed her amazement by taking it out and moving it somewhere nearer the top.

'She's rather too sure of her opinions,' Sam went on. 'It would be unkind to call her obstinate, so let's say that I don't think she knows how to adapt. To see a girl of that age who can't adapt is ridiculous, or perhaps it's sad, I don't know which.'

He shook himself, as though he was emerging from cold water. But his dissatisfaction remained, not less so when he had a chance of a word with Dr Vogel. The doctor had been on a tour of the regional centres, where, in spite of his goodwill, he had caused as much distress as any other perfectionist.

'It's a trivial matter, I suppose, Josef, but I found it inexplicable. What it came to, really, was that she chose to set up her sense of hearing against mine. I hardly knew what to say to her. After all, perfect pitch is something you're born with, like a sense of humour. You're with me, Josef?'

Dr Vogel nodded.

'Certainly, Sam. You yourself were born with neither. But you are a fine man, a good man.'

This was the first time in his life – since Dr Vogel was accepted as infallible – that Sam Brooks had ever been obliged to change his opinion of himself. The experience did not make him less self-centred, but the centre of gravity shifted. He now declared that he had no ear at all for music, and couldn't be expected to have, he was an engineer and an administrator, nothing more than that. But generosity and selfishness are not incompatible, and his need to give and share would not quite settle down with the knowledge that he had been unjust to Annie. After all, where could his juniors, those beginners in life, look for a moral example, if not to him? It was strange that Sam, who forgot unacceptable incidents with such rapidity and skill, could not quite get over this one. Mrs Milne, for example, thought it strange.

Annie, on the other hand, remembered how RPD had looked without his glasses, and wished that she hadn't been obliged to say that the singer had been flat from the E onwards, though, really, there'd been no help for it. It didn't upset her that she seemed to be in disgrace; it was just that without his glasses it seemed cruel, and even wrong, to take him aback.

'You did right to say what you thought, though,' Vi told her. 'It's no use making yourself a doormat, like Lise Bernard.'

The two of them had been on late shift. They were lying on their metal bunks, one up, one down, in the concert-hall. It was not much use trying to get to sleep. Total blackout was Security's rule, and since the tickets didn't bear numbers, and couldn't have been read if they had, newcomers clambered and felt about in search of an empty corner, swarming across the others like late returners to a graveyard before cockcrow. Time, indeed, was the great concern. The sleepers were obscurely tormented by the need to be somewhere in five, ten, or twenty minutes. Awakened, quite often, by feet walking over them, they struck matches whose tiny flames wavered in every corner of the concert-hall, and had a look at their watches, just to be sure. Yet some slept on, and the walls, designed to give the best possible acoustics for classical music, worked just as well for snoring. Accommodation, who had provided so much, had never thought of this. No barracks or dormitory in the country produced snoring of such broad tone, and above that distinctly rose the variations of the overwrought, the junior announcers rehearsing their cues, correcting themselves and starting again, continuity men suddenly shouting: '. . . and now, in a lighter mood . . .', and every now and then a fit of mysterious weeping.

'I often wonder if Lise ever came in here or not,' said Vi. Annie craned over from the top bunk. In the next tier a middle-aged secretary began to sing in her sleep. Perhaps, like Della, she had always wanted to do so. The concert-hall encouraged such dreams.

'Why are you always on about her?' Annie whispered. 'This Lise, I mean. From all you've told me, if she finds things hard again she'll get hold of you quick enough.'

Vi acknowledged this, but it was troublesome about the missing CH ticket. They were asking for it back, and, if she had to tell lies, she didn't particularly want them to be for Lise's sake.

It worried her also that RPD seemed to have taken against Annie. Who was to eat the double cheese sandwiches now, and to listen to his woes? Annie was a real help both at home and at work, but in this one respect her coming had made no difference, worse than none. The whole Seraglio's task still lay on Vi's shoulders.

Vi, however, resembled her mother, and made her mother's mistakes, in calculating only from what she had known so far. Indeed, there is always a kind of comfort in doing this. But overnight, or so it seemed, the continuity was broken and the Department changed.

The juniors, Willie and Teddy as well as the girls, had been used to a patriarchal tyranny, where they might be summoned at any time by the thunder of their Director, but were conscious of his direct protection, always within touch of his hand. Suddenly, RPD ceased to take any notice of them. He recalled that he had, like everyone else of his grade except DPP, assistant administrators and executives of various kinds, who had got used to functioning almost entirely on their own. Now they were flattered by consultations, and by two meetings within one week. The engineers had always been close to his heart, but now members of staff who had never been asked for an opinion before, and scarcely knew that they had one, were called upon to give it. They sent in suggestions for reorganizing the work, which Mrs Milne filed. Meanwhile the crazy nursery-tale atmosphere, the bear turned prince who could be led only by a maiden or a child, had disappeared, perhaps for ever.

The effect on the RPAs, reduced to their own tiny world, was curious. They were overawed. For the first time they looked at their Director from a distance and realized, almost with disbelief, how much he really had to do. Toiling up and down the first three floors of BH, humble servants of the discs, they were conscious of how far the work stretched beyond them. There were the mobile units in Egypt, there were the tireless wax cylinders which recorded the world's broadcasts, a hundred and fifty thousand words to be monitored every day. All of these depended on Sam Brooks, who not so long ago had been glad to go to sleep on Vi's shoulder.

'You'll never really get to know RPD now,' Willie told Annie. They were in a little room like a cupboard behind the ticker-tapes, which seemed not to be used for anything; he had brought a chair in there, and was cutting her hair. Willie believed that it was his duty to learn to do these things – the Red Cross Certificate had been only the first on his list – against the day when Broadcasting House was in a state of siege. At the moment he was not much of a hairdresser. A haze of snipped curls lay on the floor, and Annie's hair looked somewhat ragged.

'It doesn't matter, it'll find its own level,' she told him reassuringly.

She minded the withdrawal of RPD less than the others. After all, she'd only spoken to him the once.

Annie was absorbed, too, in those first weeks, with the discovery made by so many of those whom the chances of war swept into Broadcasting House; there was music everywhere, just for the asking. You could borrow records from the Library and find somewhere to play them, or walk into a studio and find someone else playing them. At any moment of the twenty-four hours you could listen. Round every corner Schubert sang, or Debussy murmured on the horizon, or Liszt descended in a shower of sparkling drops. Annie had heard scarcely any of this before. Sometimes she hardly wanted to go back to Hammersmith; she felt as though she was drowning.

'Didn't you get any music in Birmingham?' asked Eddie Waterlow.

'There's a greater variety of concerts than in any place in England,' said Annie stoutly, 'but my aunt didn't care for them, and my father never took me, except to *Messiah* at Christmas and *Elijah* in summer.'

'Couldn't you go on your own?'

'I hadn't the sense. I'm beginning to see that now.'

'Didn't you sing, Annie?'

'Only in choir.'

Eddie opened her mouth caressingly with the end of a chinagraph pencil.

'Untrained! You will sing the high E for me, Trilby, Treelbee!'

Annie wasn't put out by his ways any longer. She thought he was probably a bit too much on his own.

'What were you going to play? Oh, Dvaw-aw-rzhak.' He liked to imitate the Pronunciation Section. 'No, my dear, I don't think so. Perhaps one should be grateful that there haven't been any peasants in England for centuries, and if there had been they wouldn't have sung and danced. Let me look at the Mood Label, ". . . the dance grows wilder and wilder, and at length the Devil laughs, with sinister effect . . .", no, no, my dear, put it by. Refine yourself a little every day, that is my rule. I want you to learn how to listen to a whisper. Less is more! Annie, listen to less with me.'

He sent Dvorak spinning into a bin. They sat down to hear Fauré's Dolly Suite, two pianos nodding together through the afternoon, and the perpetually moving sadly unemphatic white sounds of Satie's *Socrate*.

'Have you ever shaken a concert pianist's hand when he comes off the platform?' Eddie asked her.

Annie shook her head.

'There's no strength left in that hand at all! It hangs down like this from the wrist! All used up, all!'

He was half disappointed when she asked him to play the Satie again, but at this stage of her life Annie liked everything. Most seriously he warned her that emotion must never intrude. If she ever had any strong feelings, let

87

us say strong personal affection, she mustn't let that attach itself to the music. The subject of music was music, he told her.

The other juniors were also fond of music, and Teddy was an ambitious trumpet-player, but Annie's intoxication was rather beyond them.

'She's single-minded,' suggested Willie, who was unusual in appreciating his own qualities in other people.

'That ought to make her understand RPD,' said Vi.

'He's changed,' said Teddy. 'That's a frequent phenomenon with men in middle life. Religion sometimes does it.'

Yet Sam Brooks had not changed. He enjoyed playing at being what he really was, and in altering the Department's routine he was playing directors. But he retained the great accumulation of grievances which was in fact one of his sources of nourishment, arising, as it did, not from envy but from indignation at the blindness and deafness of all around him. The new RPA had, perhaps, not been quite deaf enough, but he didn't intend to think about that again. It was almost the only annoyance that he did not mention to DPP.

Jeff was now in the front line of the BBC's defence against the Ministries, Civil Defence, Supply, Economic Warfare, Food, Salvage, who riddled the Corporation with demands for more time on the air. Before the Home News they fell back, knowing it to be hallowed ground, but every other programme, and particularly those that might entertain the listeners, were required to give way at once. Poor Eddie Waterlow's *France Fights On* was only the first of the fallen. Instructions to the public and hints – for example, towards saving tea, by using the tea-leaves twice – should, the Ministries felt, take precedence over all. The Director of Programme Planning might, in fact, have been felt to be fully employed, and yet Jeff was not surprised when Sam burst into his office.

'Jeff, I want to put this to you, as one of my oldest friends.'

'Surely you must have older friends than I am,' Jeff protested. Their life in BH had become so secluded and so strange that it was difficult to remember at times where wives or friends could come from. However, Sam was just old enough to have been shipped out to France at the end of 1917. What had become of his cronies from the last war? But Sam, unlike every other contemporary, couldn't remember much about the trenches. He'd devised a double spring for the Company's gramophone, he knew that, so that records would play twice as long; the Commanding Officer had been delighted, but then, they had had only one record, *A Little Bit of Fluff*, the three cracks endlessly holding it up in the same three places, and blame for the tedium, Sam thought, had most unjustly been transferred to him. The Company had passed a vote of thanks to the Germans when the gramophone was caught by shrapnel.

'I've never seen one like it before or since,' Sam remarked. 'It had something in common with the Blattnerphone.'

Still, why were they talking about the last war? Experience must be shared, and he believed his oldest friend would want to enter into his new distress. He had been at long last to inspect the Indispensable Emergency Personnel Quarters and found that his Department had been allocated something not much bigger than a coop. They would have to share washing facilities with Stores, Bookings and Long Term Contracts, but that would only mean a few reasonable adjustments. The point he wanted to make was that there was no provision for his four turntables. Room must be found; perhaps, after all, all this washing wasn't necessary.

'Have you spoken to Accommodation?'

'I'm not satisfied with their replies. What's more, I'm being kept in the dark again. The bells!'

In the event of an enemy landing, church bells would warn the nation. Silent now for many months, they would be rung out in case of danger from every parish. The BBC had decided that it would be enough to supplement them with ordinary commercial recordings. Jeff thought that it would be better to tell Sam about this some other time.

8

Suddenly Sam Brooks' designs came right, both for the forty-pound mobile recording equipment and the microphone windshield. It was almost as if the war was won. All the four juniors were summoned. Their Director was going to celebrate, he was going to take them out to dinner.

'It's impossible for all of them to be off duty together, Mr Brooks,' Mrs Milne pointed out. 'You're aware of that, naturally.'

'Tell Spender to find out what their duties are and look after the discs for a couple of hours, about eight till ten this evening.'

'Mr Spender is a Permanent, Grade 3.'

'Well, it won't hurt him. It will familiarize him with the juniors' work.'

Mrs Milne reminded him that Spender had been an RPA himself for several years before reaching his present position.

'That'll make it all the easier for him,' said Sam.

Mrs Milne could hardly have explained, even to herself, why she was opposed to the whole scheme, or why, now that it appeared inevitable, she had to concern herself so much with the details.

'Lyons in Piccadilly would do very nicely for them, Mr Brooks. They serve a cold baked potato there now, you know, instead of bread, to beat the shortages. Sometimes you have to queue for a while, but a baked potato is very filling.'

'Book me a table at Prunier's,' Sam replied.

He disappeared immediately with his drawings, surrounded by engineers.

At the two o'clock changeover Mrs Milne summoned the RPAs to her office, to learn of their good fortune.

'This is a very well-known restaurant, a French res-

90

taurant, and you must all of you consider your appearance.'

She was falling imperceptibly into the tone of a Victorian housekeeper inspecting the slaveys.

'Of course, some people think that, with Hitler at our gates, there shouldn't be any of this luxurious and rather ostentatious eating out, particularly perhaps in the evening. We're all of us asked to economize in our own way. The Governors were served with dried egg pasty at their last Board Meeting.'

'They got whisky, too,' said Teddy. 'I saw it going up.'

'I wish you were coming with us, Mrs Milne,' Annie said, turning, on an impulse, towards her. Mrs Milne saw that she meant it, and if any one of the others had made the suggestion it would have been quite gratifying. They, after all, were in a sense children of the regiment, they had come before the cold winter of 1939 and were known all over the building; the boys, not really fully grown yet, were patted on the head and given small coins by Dr Vogel. Then she reminded herself, but not because she had forgotten it, that Annie Asra had been her own appointment. Mary Staples had referred to it only the other day, as a proof of how well things could be managed if all the interviewing was left to the two of them.

Before leaving the office, Mrs Milne always arranged a candle and a box of matches, half open, with one match taken out and laid diagonally across the box, on RPD's desk. This was in case the power failed and he needed a light in a hurry. She had never managed to get him to take very much interest in the arrangement, but it was the last thing she had to do before she left. Willing to extend her control for a little longer, she traced RPD to the fifth floor and asked what he intended to do about transport.

'Tell DPP I'll need his taxi,' said Sam impatiently.

DPP's taxi-driver allowed all five of them to get inside, Willie being small, and destined to provide exceptions.

Regent Street was closed to traffic while the shop fronts were being reinforced, so they went round by Marble Arch. There had been showers all day. In Green Park the barrage balloons were going up in a flock through the tepid evening sky, while inside the taxi a pastoral atmosphere also reigned, the juniors content with their newly restored guardian.

'They cost £500 each, you know, Mr Brooks,' said Willie, gazing at the silver-fleeced balloons, which seemed to be fixed and grazing in the upper air. 'It's going to be a serious matter if we lose two or three of those.'

In St James's they got out and waited on the pavement while the taxi was paid off, then entered the grand restaurant through whose doors came a whiff of the lost smell of Paris. Inside the brownish glitter of the two mirrored walls reflected a heroic display which rejected the possibility of change. Even the diners, many of them in uniform, seemed to have escaped time. Some of them could have sat opposite Clemençeau or Robert St. Loup, and one, with his great starched napkin at the ready, might almost have been General Pinard.

Willie lingered rather behind the others, talking to the sedate commissionaire in his *chocolat au lait*-coloured uniform. Then he came confidently over to their corner table.

'Mrs Milne thought we wouldn't know how to behave in a place like this,' he observed.

'I'm not sure that you do,' Vi said quietly. 'What were you talking about to that man at the door?'

'I was asking him if he'd seen Frédé. I described him as well as I could from what you told me. After all, a chap like that must see a lot of Frenchmen come and go.'

'Frédé wouldn't ever come to a place like this, it's expensive.'

'French people spend a remarkably high proportion of their income on food,' said Willie seriously.

'Well, he's not spending it over here, anyway. You didn't see him. He couldn't wait to get rid of Lise and be off.'

Teddy was talking to RPD about wine, and, by a method as old as Socrates, was made to feel that he had chosen the champagne which they eventually ordered. Annie looked at de Gaulle's proclamations, pasted to the walls of the beautiful shadowy room. I'm beginning to know those by heart, she thought.

Prunier's were inclined to think that it must be a First Communion outing. There was a spirit of indulgence suitable to a godfather in the way the host demanded the best there was, and then, as it happened, Annie was wearing a white dress. It was, in fact, one she'd been obliged to get for choir competitions, in a style not likely to have been chosen by anyone but the Vicar's wife, with a view to Christmas and to further competitive events, and made in white silk from Anstruthers' Fabric Hall. She wouldn't have put it on if Mrs Simmons hadn't taken it out, and exclaimed, and insisted that it would only take her ten minutes to iron it, though in fact it came to much more like half an hour. Of course, she had to wear it then. The white dress caused the head waiter to place her on Mr Brooks' right.

Boiled lobsters came, and the table was almost hidden by the fringed sea creatures, resting between their cracked tails. None of the juniors liked the taste of them fresh. Seaweed and a taste of drains, thought Vi. But they bent their faces low, their sensations must not be guessed, and Sam, who deceived himself so often, was easily deceived by these children. They worked together as though following an unseen cue, one of them talking while the others con-cealed the bits and pieces, with tactful haste, under the lobster's carapace on their plates.

'They plunge them head first into boiling salted water,' declared Willie. 'That instantly destroys life.'

'I've done it often enough with shrimps,' said Vi, 'but it's hard to tell whether they've gone in head first or not.'

She had intended to check Willie when they got to the restaurant, but by now she felt that it wasn't worth while. Champagne is bought and drunk to lead to such changes of mind, and Vi had drunk three-quarters of a glass. So too had Teddy.

'I want you to know that I'll always treasure this moment,' he said suddenly. 'Land, sea, or air, I don't know where, But when the sad thought comes to you, Be sure that I'm remembering too.' While Teddy half-rose to his feet, toasting his own certainty of living for ever, the debris on the table was swept away and replaced by a beautiful red currant tart.

The waiter described a flourish with his tongs over the melting crust. Like all good waiters he was a fine adjuster of relationships, particularly when children were to be served, and he estimated the RPAs as that. Children had to be addressed with an eye on the adult who was paying for them, but directly, too, as from one who had a family to support at home.

'You are the youngest, you do not mind being served last?' he asked, poised over Willie with a fatherly smile.

'Perhaps, since you've put that question, you'd like my considered opinion,' Willie replied, 'I don't just mean on the comparatively trivial matter of eldest and youngest. When peace comes I think it shouldn't be too difficult to get the governments of the world to consent to my scheme of alternative roles for all human beings. It's generally accepted already that if everyone were to eat one day and have nothing at all on the next we could ensure world plenty. But I'd like to see more than that. Those who serve and those who are served would also change places in strict rotation, so that to-morrow evening, for example, you in your turn would be waited upon.'

Vi roused herself. 'I shouldn't like to be here when you're doing the serving, Willie. There'd be long delays all round.' She added, as kindly as she could, 'You shouldn't go on like that, he's got other tables to look after.'

Willie turned red. 'I can be thoughtless at times,' he said.

Their Director gave them all a little more champagne, ignoring the just perceptible hint not to do this, sketched by the retreating waiter. The infants are getting overexcited, his shoulders said. And now Sam, leaning back in his chair and filling such a noticeable space, began to exert a natural power which few people had ever seen, but which answered in human terms to his ability with electrical equipment. Some of the same qualities are needed to organise people and things, and though Sam did not understand his juniors, he knew how to make them happy. Without even noticing Willie's embarrassment of a few moments ago, he conjured it away. He told them stories, delaying as he drew near to an end so that they were on the verge of seeing too well what was going to happen next, then pausing and asking them if they'd like to finish for him, but they were under a spell, and could not. In these engrossing tales Eddie Waterlow appeared, and the Director General, and the last-minute removal of drunken commentators from the microphone, and the sad deafening of Dr Vogel as he knelt down to record the opening batsman at Old Trafford. Lured into the circle of words, knowing how much he was putting himself out, they felt themselves truly his guests, ready to do anything for him. Teddy's laughter must have been some of the loudest ever heard at Prunier's.

Annie's eyes were bright and her attention was almost painful, but she did not laugh as much as the others. It was not her way. That would not quite do for Sam, and without leaving the rest of them he turned to his right and concentrated his whole attention for a moment on her. She looked back at him fearlessly, sitting solid and composed in her peculiar white dress.

'Are you enjoying yourself?'

Annie nodded, but that was not enough for him.

'You know, I've remembered now what it is, I mean who it is, you remind me of, Annie. It's a French picture by Monet, or Manet, it doesn't really matter which, a girl, or perhaps a boy, dressed in white, and sitting at a café table, all in shade, under a striped awning, but there's very bright sunshine beyond that, and there's some older people at the table too, with glasses of something in front of them, wine

I suppose, but none of them are really looking at each other.'

'I'm sorry you don't know whether it was a boy or a girl,' said Annie mildly. He saw that she had not given in.

'You haven't been with us as long as the others. I should like. . . .' He was improvising. 'I should like to give you a present. The best! There's no point at all in a present unless it's the best one can give.'

'I don't know what the best would be, Mr Brooks.' She was not worried.

It was a game.

'I shall give you a ring.'

They had all of them been with him in the studio and knew how dexterous he was, but none of them would have believed that he could take the inch of gold wire still dangling from the champagne bottle, pierce the end through one of the red currants and give it three twists or flicks so that the currant was transfixed, a jewel on which the blond light shone. His broad fingers held the wire as neatly as a pair of pliers.

'Well, Annie.'

Annie had been keeping her hands under the table, but now she spread them out on the stiff-feeling tablecloth. They were pinkish and freckled, but delicate, not piano-player's hands, not indeed as practical as one would have expected, thin and tender. After some hesitation, as though making a difficult selection, Sam Brooks picked up the left hand and most ingeniously put the currant ring onto the third finger, compressing it to make it fit exactly.

The others watched in silence. Annie did not know what to say or do, so she said nothing, and left her hand where it was on the table. Something inside her seemed to move and unclose.

At that precise moment, while the juniors were eating their dessert at Prunier's, Annie fell in love with RPD absolutely, and hers must have been the last generation to fall in love without hope in such an unproductive way. After the war the species no longer found it biologically useful, and indeed it was not useful to Annie. Love without hope grows in its own atmosphere, and should encourage the imagination, but Annie's grew narrower. She exerted the utmost of her will-power to this end. She never pictured herself trapped in the main lift with Mr Brooks above the third floor, or of rescuing him from a burning building or a Nazi parachutist or even a mad producer armed with a shotgun. He existed, and so did she, and she had perhaps sixty years left to put up with it, although her father died at fifty-six. She was in love, as she quite saw, with a middle-aged man who said the same thing to all the girls, who had been a prince for an evening which he'd most likely forgotten already, who had given her a ring with a red currant in it and who cared, to the exclusion of all else, for his work. As a result, it was generally understood, Mrs Brooks had left him, and the thought of his loneliness made her heart contract as though squeezed by a giant hand; but then you couldn't really pretend that he *was* lonely, and so Annie didn't pretend. This, of course, meant that she suffered twice, and she failed to reckon the extra cost of honesty.

The truth was that she was almost too well trained in endurance, having drawn since birth on the inexhaustible fund of tranquil pessimism peculiar to the English Midlands. Her father's friends, who came round evenings and sat in their accustomed chairs, speaking at long intervals, said 'We're never sent more than we can bear', and 'You begin life helpless, and you end it helpless', and 'Love breaks the heart, porridge breaks the wind', and when she worked at Anstruthers' hosiery counter they hadn't asked the customers whether they wanted plain knit or micro-mesh, but 'Do you want the kind that ladders, or the kind that goes into holes?' These uncompromising alternatives were not intended to provide comfort, only self-respect.

Annie – although she also knew that those who don't speak have to pay it off in thinking – was resolved on silence. Whatever happened, and after all she was obliged to see Mr Brooks two or three times every day, though she by no means looked forward to it, feeling herself more truly alive when she could picture him steadily without seeing him – whatever happened, he needn't know how daft she was. But words were scarcely necessary in the closeness of the RPA room. They all knew how it was with her there.

Vi wanted to be of help, but it was difficult to find facts which Annie had not already faced.

'He's old, Annie,' she ventured at last.

'He is,' Annie replied calmly, 'he's forty-six: I looked him up in the BBC Handbook, and it's my opinion that he's putting on weight. I daresay he wouldn't look much in bed.'

'But what do you expect to come of it?'

'Nothing.'

Vi felt troubled. She was conscious, as she sometimes was when Willie Sharpe was talking, of a sort of wrong-headed dignity, and she had a conviction, too, that relationships could not be altered to such an extent as this, and that RPD was simply not there to be fallen in love with. 'It's not right,' she thought, feeling guilty, at the same time, of her own good luck in life. A few nights ago, just when Annie happened to be on night shift and she had her room to herself, Chris had turned up. He had docked at Liverpool with forty-eight hours leave, got the train as far as Rugby, been shunted off into a siding because of an air-raid warning and told they would stay there till morning, taken a lift with an army convoy to Luton, another one to Woolwich, and a third on a potato lorry to Covent Garden, and then, since it was in the small hours, walked the last eight miles to Hammersmith, climbed up the back of the house by way of the coal-shed, opened her window, got in under the sheets and when she'd nearly jumped out of her skin said, in quite the old way: 'There's no need to be surprised, you're quite a nice-looking girl.' Next morning her mother, when told Chris had arrived for breakfast, had made no comment, and it struck Vi that this too might have been much the same in 1914.

Why couldn't things be as simple as that for everybody? Teddy suggested that they might consult the Readers Problems in the *Mirror*. The answers column, conducted by the Two Old Codgers, he'd been told, had saved many from desperation and worse. He'd just set out the problem clearly, altering the names, of course, and the ages, and the addresses, and where they worked, and what they did. Vi had no patience with him sometimes.

Willie, saddened by the experience in which Annie seemed to be trapped without escape, took her to task.

'It's wrong, because your situation isn't natural. I've worked that out to my own satisfaction.'

'I can't get it to go away, though. Doesn't that make it natural?'

They were checking each other's time sheets before going down to tea.

'Love is of the body and the spirit,' Willie told her earnestly, 'and there's no real difference between them.'

'If you say that, you can't ever have seen anyone die,' said Annie. And indeed at this time he never had.

Mrs Milne, to whom no-one had given any kind of hint, must have learned through listening to the air itself what she would never have been willingly told. The Old Servants had developed a sixth sense in these matters. It occurred to her that it was her duty to speak to RPD.

Speaking, in this sense, was undertaken only at a ceremonial time, when the day's letters were brought in for signature, and there was also a set rhetorical form, beginning with observations of general and even national interest and coming gradually to the particular. Mrs Milne, therefore, rustling in at five o'clock, began by asking whether he'd heard that members of the Stock Exchange had opened a book and were quoting odds on how many enemy aircraft were shot down each day, and what kind of mentality, when you came to think of it, did that show, and whether he'd noticed the acute shortage of kippers which made it well-nigh impossible to offer traditional hospitality to overnight visitors. It was different, of course, for those who could afford to frequent restaurants. These subjects were singularly ill-chosen and showed Mrs Milne to be in a state of nervous tension. Sam made no pretence of listening until she said:

'Mr Brooks, I should like to have a word with you about Miss Asra.'

'I can't think why. When I tried to talk to you about her before you told me she was a very usual-looking girl from the Midlands.'

He scrawled his signature several times. 'What's she been doing?'

It was very unlike him to remember any remark she had made more than a few hours ago.

'It might be better for everyone . . .' she said, her voice scarcely audible now.

Her Director stared at her coldly.

'I think that Miss Asra is alone in the world, except for an aunt,' she went on resolutely. 'The girl must feel lonely, and her aunt must miss her a great deal.'

'Is her aunt alone in the world too?' enquired Sam. 'There can't be as many people in Birmingham as I thought.'

Mrs Milne tried again.

'Of course, Miss Asra won't be due for any annual leave until she has been with us for a year, but, in view of the emergency and her special circumstances we might make an exception in her case, a kind of prolonged compassionate leave, if you follow me.'

'I don't follow you in the least. If you're interested in Annie's aunt you have my full permission to get in touch with her.' He shovelled the heap of letters towards her. 'Has Annie said she wanted to go away?'

'Not exactly.'

'Tell me when she says so exactly.'

Annie had various methods, besides the control of her imagination, for maintaining proper pride. Sometimes she spoke

100

to herself in the third person, as the organist at St Martin's used to speak, when flustered, to the choir. 'Asra, are you with me?' 'Dobbs, you've no need to glance so frequently as Asra.' Asra, she said to herself, running for the Hammersmith bus, you don't mean any more to him that the furniture does. And that was really a good comparison. He'd subside and lean against you and tell you all those difficulties about the European and Far Eastern sections, and you could feel his weight lying there, just as if you were the back of a chair. She'd no call to be surprised at this, Vi had told her about it when she came, only at first he hadn't taken to her, now he had, but it was no-one's fault but her own if she was cut to the heart. If you can't face living your life day by day, you must live it minute by minute. At least, thank God, her aunt had gone overseas with the ATS and she'd no obligation to leave London. She was free to stay here and be unhappy, just so long as she didn't become ridiculous; for that she didn't think she could forgive herself.

'Your nose is cold,' said Eddie Waterlow, pressing it with his forefinger as she sat listening to music, his touch light as a fall of dust. 'That is a sign of health in pets, so you are not actually out of condition. Something is amiss, however. How are you getting gon?'

Mr Waterlow was the only person she had ever met who imitated her voice, the scrupulously fair intonation of Selly Oak, neither rising nor falling, giving each syllable its equal weight, as though considering its feelings before leaving it behind, and lingering over the final one so that it is given the opportunity to start the next word also. With so many more obtrusive voices around him, so many much more decisive accents, he was fascinated, as a connoisseur, by the gentle transitions, said to be the most difficult in the English language to imitate exactly, getting gon, going gon, passing gon. Curiously enough, she did not mind this at all.

'I'm getting on very nicely,' she said.

'No, no, you are not. You are not wanted as you should be, not appreciated as you wish, in this like me, in this very much like me.'

'My God, Mr Waterlow,' said Annie sadly. Does everybody in Broadcasting House know how daft I am?'

He told her that she was betraying herself, and of course at the same time indulging herself, by playing Tschaikovsky. They had to adjourn to one of the canteen store-rooms where there was an old upright piano, long since retired from the struggle to divide the air into music, and a whole tone flat in the middle register. There it was Satie again, and to oblige him she tried one of the little cabaret songs, but could hardly make herself heard above his instructions.

'Ah yes . . . *modestement* . . . for the nerves . . . just let it be a simple occurrence, no logic, just let it happen, however strangely . . . a little incongruity, please, "owl steals pince-nez of Wolverhampton builder" . . . sing, Annie, sing . . . like a nightingale, a nighting gale, with toothache . . . "I command removal from my presence sadness, silence and dolorous meditation". . . .'

'I can't imagine how you get through the day without anything to do, Mr Waterlow,' Annie said, when he had reverently shut the lid of the dejected piano, 'I've never met a man before who didn't have to work hard.'

Eddie spread out his arms, as one who was ready at any time for the call.

'Surely the BBC can find something for you?' she asked gently. He looked forlorn.

'The BBC is doing gits bit. We put out the truth, but only contingent truth, Annie! The opposite could also be true! We are told that German pilots have been brought down in Croydon and turned out to know the way to the post- office, that Hitler has declared that he only needs three fine days to defeat Great Britain, and that there is an excellent blackberry crop and therefore it is our patriotic duty to make jam. But all this need not have been true, Annie! If the summer had not been fine, there might have been no blackberries.'

'Of course there mightn't,' said Annie. 'You're just

making worries for yourself, Mr Waterlow. There isn't anything at all that mightn't be otherwise. After all, I mightn't have . . . what I mean is, how can they find anything to broadcast that's got to be true, and couldn't be anything else?'

He gestured towards the piano.

'We couldn't put out music all day!'

'Music and silence.'

After she had gone back on shift, Eddie thought for a while about Sam Brooks. There was something magnificent after all, in the way he squandered young people and discarded them and looked round absent-mindedly for more. It implied great faith in his own future. But should his attention be drawn, perhaps, to Annie's case?

By the end of August the heavy raids had begun. Vi and Annie were both out when the Simmons' house in Hammersmith was knocked down. Mrs Simmons and the children were quite all right, having taken shelter under the hall table, a half-size billiard table really, which was of a quality you couldn't get nowadays if you tried. Mr Simmons had to stay to look after the shop, but the family left London, and Vi went with them. Annie got accommodation at the YMCA hostel opposite Westminster Abbey; Mr Simmons brought up her things in his van, and she knew he was kindly using some of the petrol ration which he got for the business. It was only her clothes, really, covered now with flakes of plaster. It was just as well that she had brought so little with her in the first place.

Vi wrote to say that her wedding day was fixed, she was going up to Liverpool some time in September to marry Chris and to be his till the end of Life's Story. She wished she'd been able to invite them all, but they'd have a reunion after the war when the lights went up again, they must all swear to make a note of it, August the 30th by the Edith Cavell statue off Trafalgar Square, the side marked Fidelity. The letter did not sound quite like the Vi they had known, and made her seem farther away.

103

9

After the first week of September London became every morning a somewhat stranger place. The early morning sound was always of glass being scraped off the pavement. The brush hissed and scraped, the glass chattered, tinkled, and fell. Lyons handed out cold baked potatoes through one hole in their windows and took in the money through another. The buses, diverted into streets for which they were not intended, seemed to take the licence of a dream, drawing up on the pavements and nosing against front windows to look in at the startled inhabitants. A number 113 became seriously wedged against DPP's taxi in Riding House Street and volunteers were needed to dislodge it. They returned to Broadcasting House white with dust. The air in fact was always full of this fine, whitish dust which was suspended in the air and settled slowly, long after the buildings fell.

More menacing than the nightly danger was the need to find a willing listener for bomb stories the next morning. Little incidents of the raids, or of the journey to work, were met and countered at the office by other little incidents, and fell back rebuffed. But all new societies are quick to establish the means of exchange. After Mrs Staples had described how the contents of her handbag, keys, throat lozenges and all, had been sucked, rather than blown, away from her, and how she'd not been allowed to smoke all evening because of the broken gas mains, Mrs Milne felt entitled to a question of her own; if things were going on like this – and she had several anecdotes in reserve – wouldn't it be wise to send one's nice things away to some safer part of the country?

'I'm sure it would,' said Mrs Staples, 'if you can find someone you can trust to look after them.'

'I can't get RPD to consider the question at all. He doesn't even seem to know whether he *has* any nice things or not. I daresay Mrs Brooks took most of them away with her when she left Streatham. I don't think we shall hear very much more from that quarter,' she added.

Mrs Staples considered. 'You mean specimen glass and china, and that sort of thing?'

'Yes, the irreplaceables, the things you never use – those are what really matters. I've got a damask table-cloth, you know, and napkins to match for twenty-four people. I've heard it said that a woman's possessions are part of herself. If she loses her things, her personality undergoes a change.'

'It's just that one has to be careful when living alone,' said Mrs Staples. 'When one's children are grown up or in the Forces and the flat is empty I find that one talks to certain pieces of furniture quite often, and to oneself, of course.'

'The thing is not to be too hard on oneself,' Mrs Milne replied.

DPP's economy in the matter of staff made it possible for him to avoid the morning stories and almost all discussion of the raids. Placed, as he now was, with the responsibility of making a clean sweep of the programmes at any given moment in favour of battle instructions and of the Prime Minister's new slogan 'You can always take one with you', which was to resound through every home and place of work in Great Britain as soon as the first German landed on this soil, Jeff wished that he had not run out of cigars. Mac might bring some, and he was due over in England pretty soon. He had cabled that he wanted to broadcast direct from the roof of BH, in the thick of the raids, instead of being confined with the rest of the overseas correspondents to the basement studios. There was little or no chance, however, of the Director General giving way on this point, and Jeff idly pictured himself wrestling with Mac on the stairs, as in a silent film, to prevent him going any higher, while Nazi assault troops pounded out of the lifts. Perhaps we all ought to be in the movies, he thought.

Barnett, on one of his regular calls, told Jeff that America was drawing nearer to the brink of war. Lines of exhaustion showed clearly on his face, which was creased like the dry bed of a river. 'The way I look at it is this. The day the United States declare war on Nazi Germany, the Central and South American republics will follow suit. Well, excluding British Guiana and British Honduras, that gives you by my reckoning fifteen independent countries that are going to come in on our side. Now, Mr Haggard, all of them are going to want representation at the BBC. That in its turn means fifteen new sections, and although the standards of living in those places varies, I believe, and their governments are none too stable, they'll all of them want carpets, chairs, desks, typewriters adapted to the Spanish alphabet and steel filing cabinets. If you can tell me where to get any more steel filing cabinets measuring up to our specifications, Mr Haggard, I'm prepared to go to bed with Hitler's grandmother.'

'I hadn't thought of the position exactly in that way,' Jeff replied.

'I daresay you hadn't, very few have. Decisions are made, as you know, with very little thought as to how they're to be carried out.'

'You have my sympathy.'

'But what do you suggest I should do?'

'Pray for a negotiated peace,' said Jeff.

'Now, Mr Haggard, you don't mean that, we all know you don't mean half of what you say.'

'I don't at all mean that it would be desirable. I'm simply saying that it's the only solution for the problem of the steel filing cabinets. If you don't like the idea, you'll have to find a new approach to the whole question.'

On the night of September the 7th the BBC received the signal for 'Invasion Imminent' from the C in C Home

Forces, who now had priority over the Ministry of Information. This signal was followed by another: 'No bells to ring till advise.' By an understandable confusion, however, there were church bells which did start ringing in scattered parishes all over the country. Not one was recorded.

'We missed the lot,' Sam protested, at white heat. 'A false alarm, well, what if it was? When the real thing comes there may not be time to ring them.' He set out in search of Dr Vogel.

Hard to track down, the doctor was sometimes to be found in the Monitoring Section, where he had a relation of sorts, said to be his nephew, although he appeared rather the older of the two. The atmosphere of this section was deeply studious. High up in the building, refugee scholars in headphones, quietly clad, disguising their losses, transcribed page after page of Nazi broadcasts in a scholar's shorthand. When they broke for coffee, Beethoven's last quartets were played. Even Sam, fuming energetically into the room, was checked for a moment. Then he recollected himself and shouted: 'Heinz Vogel! Is there anyone here called Heinz Vogel? I'm looking for Josef.'

A bent figure lifted its head. 'Unfortunately my uncle has died.'

Dr Vogel, killed by a piece of flying drainpipe, had been one of the BBC's first casualties. And after all he had not been trying to record. Standing among the debris, he had been courteously persuading an ARP warden, on behalf of a complete stranger, that it was legal under the emergency regulations for a householder to return twice to his ruined dwelling, once for his mattress, and once for his personal effects. 'The citizen has this right very clearly laid down,' he explained patiently. 'That is English law.'

Laid to rest in Golders Green, Dr Vogel had wished to be buried in his native Frankfurt. Jeff, not easily surprised, was a little taken aback when he was required to sign papers undertaking to see to this, as soon as hostilities ceased. The nephew, painfully accurate and humble, pointed out that there would be no financial obligation, indeed nothing for DPP to do at all. It was only that he himself was not a British citizen, and needed the signature and authorization of someone of a certain standing.

'What about RPD?' Jeff asked. 'He worked a good deal with your uncle, whereas I only knew him very slightly.'

'Unfortunately he was too busy.'

'Did he tell you to try me?'

'Yes, Mr Haggard, he suggested that I should make this application to you.'

Jeff, writing more carefully than usual, signed at the foot of the numerous pages, which trembled in the nephew's hand.

'Would you like a drink, Vogel?' he said. 'We all valued your uncle's work. I'm very sorry.'

Heinz Vogel thanked him profusely, but did not drink.

For some time Jeff's meditations had been following a certain course, which he felt less and less inclined to check. A few weeks at most would show whether the invasion was ever likely to take place. If it didn't, and the war expanded in quite other directions, might it not be possible to leave the problems of Sam, as well as schedules of the Home and Forces Network, to other hands? Among the documents he might hand on to a successor would be a chart of the rescue operations, great or small, necessary for getting Sam through a given period of time. And 'necessary' was not an exaggeration. Sam's methods might be improved, but his knowledge could not be replaced. It would have to be explained, for example, that this helpless and endearing expert in self-indulgence, seemingly unhinged at times, was the man who had established the apparent decrease in the proportion of higher and lower frequencies with respect to the middle range as loudspeaker level is decreased. While the war lasted, if the BBC wished to record itself, it needed Sam.

Someone must support him, then – perhaps a new

Director of Programme Planning, so that the transition would be less noticeable. Meanwhile, Jeff considered whether it was too late to save himself. Helping other people is a drug so dangerous that there is no cure short of total abstention. Mac had warned Jeff of this, and indeed he had said more; 'you're weakening these people.'

But the possibility of his doing something else had, as it happened, been manifested to Jeff like an emanation from various quarters, sometimes clear, sometimes muted, in the form of soundings-out, hints and suppositions, always guarded, because he was a linguist, and to know foreign languages can never be quite creditable, but tending steadily towards a certain point. This point was his knowledge of Turkish and Russian. There might be employment for him outside this country and outside the BBC, comparable in importance with the post he now held. It was being assumed that his Turkish was as fluent as his French.

'Well?' said Jeff.

That was the way things were done, or were put forward to be about to be done, in those days. Jeff had very little to leave behind – that too was well understood – not much to gain, either, and no embarrassments beyond a possible encounter with his former wives. He could go anywhere. He admitted that he might make better use of his detachment. A natural tendency to extravagance had prompted him to waste it, and to watch the waste with amusement. I can't change, he thought, but I can begin to withdraw.

Under a star-powdered sky the Recorded Programmes Department set up an open microphone on the roof of BH, which caught every sound of the raids until the last enemy aircraft departed into silence. On the roof, too, the parts of the rifle were named to Teddy and Willie by Reception from the main desk of BH, who told them frequently, as he looked down at the pale pink smoke of London's fires, that it reminded him of a quiet sector of the line in the last show. Most of the staff juniors attended, and sometimes Reception would sit and play poker with them for margarine coupons, while the Regent's Park guns rocked them like ship's boys aloft.

It felt odd to go down from the roof, during that cloudless autumn, into the interior of BH, where the circulation had become even more complex now that on receipt of the second, or purple, warning all personnel had to leave their rooms and proceed by the quickest route to the basement. It was only the fact that very few of them actually did this that kept the administration going. The Monitoring Section, for example, never raised their heads from their grave task.

Establishment had expected that as soon as Vi Simmons had gone, they would get an application for a further supply of RPAs, but none came. There was extra work, which Annie was quite prepared to do. But time, as though in revenge for the minute watch that was kept on it, from the early news till *Lighten Our Darkness*, behaved oddly, so that she felt much older than she really was, and as though she had been with the BBC much longer than she really had. And yet Willie and Teddy, veterans of nearly eight months, spoke of epochs which she had never known. Once, when the engineers were testing the line from Manchester, a succulent voice cut in, singing an approximation of *Look For the Silver Lining*.

'That's Della!'

In the middle of the second refrain the singer was abruptly switched off. 'Well, at least she's been recorded,' said Willie.

In spite of herself Annie could not help asking: 'Did she get on well with RPD?'

Willie thought not. They were too much alike, he told her.

With only three of them left, the concept of the Seraglio seemed lost. Sam no longer sent for Annie to come and sit with him, but wandered about the building, when the need arose, until he found her. Then, of course, she was rarely

110

alone. It was impossible to maintain the old shifts, and they got through the work as best they could.

'There's something wrong with these,' she said to Teddy, as they sorted out the discs of *Children Calling Home*. These were recorded by line from families evacuated to Canada and the United States. The children's bewilderment, they remembered, had often made Vi feel like crying.

Teddy wearily put one of them onto the turntable. A deep bass voice, hoarsened with smoking, began: 'Hullo, Mum and Dad and Juicy Nelly . . .'

'They're mixed up with Forces Messages again,' said Annie.

They looked dolefully at each other. It was wrong to admit, no matter what the subject, that you were losing heart. And then, when RPD bounded in, as he did at that moment, giving the effect of a trajectory fuelled by indignation and landing exactly where he had intended, their lives expanded and glowed and they knew they were too important to the Corporation ever to feel tired.

'What are you complaining about now, Mr Brooks?' asked Annie, speaking a good deal more bluntly than Vi had done, but with a radiant smile. Diverted, apparently, from his original intention, Sam looked at her and complained that her hair was ragged.

Teddy, watching him, thought: 'Perhaps I ought to break it to him that Annie fancies him.' Jeez, though, it would have to be done tactfully.

Sam twisted one of the outlying curls round his finger. 'Who's been hacking at this?' he asked.

'Willie Sharpe,' said Annie.

'He's made a mess of it.'

'He'll get better with practice.'

'You ought to have asked me about it. I'm very good at cutting hair.'

'Where did you learn, Mr Brooks?' Teddy asked in amazement. 'In the trenches?'

'No, my mother taught me when I was about ten. That

meant I could trim my father's beard for him. I imagine the idea was to save money. We weren't well off.'

The two juniors looked at each other, silenced by these impossibilities.

Then Annie felt something stronger than herself take her by the throat and said: 'Do you cut Mrs Brooks' hair?'

'You mean my wife?'

'Yes.'

He was not in the least perturbed. 'I don't think the question ever arose. She was quite self-sufficient.' The enormous moment passed without leaving a trace.

He sprang to his feet and began to pace the stuffy mixer room. 'Teddy, I ask you as man to man, do we appreciate Annie enough? Quite apart from her resemblance to that picture of a small French boy, or girl, in white which none of us seem able to identify, she is tranquil, she is steady, she isn't carried out of herself, as I am, not only by the ludicrous admistrative errors of the Corporation, but by the sheer injustice of life's coincidences. I don't suppose either of you realize that Vogel, Dr Josef Vogel, was a casualty in last Saturday's raids?'

'Yes, we did know that, Mr Brooks,' said Teddy. 'He went when there was all that damage round the Highgate Cat and Bells. We had a whip round the Department, you know, for some flowers.'

Sam ignored this. 'You understand, Annie, I think, even if no-one else does, that in his professional capacity Vogel was indispensable to me, I'd put it as strongly as that, in the whole business of catching the sound of history as it passes. I must have discussed with him a hundred times what we'd do if German troops landed. In what archives, I put it to you, will you find a recording of the first wave of an invading tank division moving up a sand and shingle beach? I'd told him I was bringing him with me on the unit and we'd place ourselves on the foreshore, or, better still, perhaps, a mile or so up the London road. I can read you the application I've made to Coastal Defence. Of course, they're trying to make needless restrictions of all kinds. . . .'

112

'RPD struck me as a bit heartless,' said Teddy, when they were left with *Children Calling Home*.

'I don't think so,' said Annie. 'Dr Vogel would have felt just the same.'

Teddy sighed. 'You won't listen to a word against him, will you?'

'I can't help myself, Teddy. I know the style he carries on, but I can't help it.'

'He gets round you. He gets round everyone.'

Annie could not explain to him why she felt no resentment. Her feeling for Mr Brooks was so much the most important part of her life that it seemed like something which did not belong to her, but which she had to carry about with her, at work or in her room, there was no difference. She had a kind of affection, too, for the love itself, which was so strong, but maintained itself on so little. There had been a time, not at all long ago, when she hadn't had this responsibility, but it was hard for her to remember how she had felt then.

Eddie Waterlow, meeting her in the corridor, looked at her sharply.

'Fly with me!' he exclaimed.

'What from, Mr Waterlow?' Annie asked, not pretending to misunderstand him.

10

On September the 15th the RAF announced that they were no longer making School Certificate a requirement for flying duties and advertised for volunteers. Willie Sharpe read this on the ticker-tape after he had done his last job for that day, delivering the recordings for *London After Dark*. It was a very bright moonlight night outside, a bad night, as it turned out, in more ways than one.

He had a ticket to sleep in the concert-hall, and a meal allowance in the canteen. On the wiped counter, stale with its twenty-four hour service, nothing was left but herrings in mustard sauce; they were the week's Patriotic Fish Dish. At separate tables, two messengers and a Czech professor of philosophy were picking quietly over their heap of bones.

Willie remembered Tad (who had recently sent Teddy a photograph of himself with a moustache, and a Polish fiancée), and then the outing to Prunier's. Soon I shan't be here, he thought. I can pass for eighteen easily. With a bit more experience of life's testing moments, I shall look eighteen and a half. He imagined himself in training, in the Mess, listening to *London After Dark*, and wondering whether anybody would be interested then if he said he'd once worked in the Corporation.

The Czech professor approached his table, and asked whether it would be possible to borrow a torch. Evidently he too was going to venture into the concert-hall.

'I'm sorry, I never carry one. As a matter of fact I'm training myself to do without a light, to make myself more useful in case of night combat.'

Willie, however, was too tired for once to expatiate on this. As the professor, resigned to refusal, moved away to ask elsewhere, he handed in his voucher and left.

The first heroic or primitive period of the concert-hall had only lasted a very short while. The grades quickly reasserted themselves, although the structure was complicated, as always, by the demands of time. Just inside the entrance, the old dressing rooms had been turned into separate cubicles for executives and senior news readers, but junior news readers (after one o'clock in the morning) and administrative assistants (on programmes of special importance) could claim to use any that were vacant.

Tonight they all seemed to be standing empty.

Willie had quite often managed to take half an hour's unentitled sleep in one of the cubicles. He hoped that it was right to regard this as training in initiative. The mattresses were really the same as all the others, but there were single beds, and even small tables. In front of each hung a curtain of a material half-way between felt and sacking, which had once been used to deaden sound in the drama studios.

He paused and listened acutely to the great ground swell of snoring. Pitched higher, pitched lower, came the familiar snatches of coloratura, swearing, and pleading, but everybody seemed safely stowed. Almost reassured, he felt his way behind the rank-smelling curtain into the thick darkness, trusting that he was in the cubicle next to the door, the best, of course, if you had to leave later in a hurry. He was frightened when he heard someone moaning in the corner.

'Who is it?' he whispered.

'Strike a match. There's some by the bed.'

He thought he recognized the voice. The match lit up part of a mottled, damp and livid face. He had always thought Lise rather pretty, she looked frightful now.

'What are you doing in there?'

There was blood on the floor, on the standard green lino which the BBC also used to deaden sound.

'Lise, have you met with an accident?'

The girl suddenly heaved over, crouching under the

regulation blanket on all fours, and swaying like an animal fit to drop.

'Shall I get you a cup of tea?' Willie asked in terror. He knew very well what was happening. Make me wrong, he prayed.

'Is this cubicle occupied?' murmured a voice, a man's voice, a foot away behind the curtain. Only an Old Servant could maintain such correctness, only a trained baritone could produce such a resonant *mezza voce*.

Willie peeped out. It was as he well knew, John Haliburton, the Senior Announcer.

'I rather thought I heard a woman's voice in here. But if it's empty. . . .'

The Halibut was carrying a kind of dark lantern, and wore the correctly creased uniform of the BBC's Defence Volunteers. Everybody knew, although he himself never mentioned it, that he had been wounded at Le Cateau and should be allowed to rest whenever possible. Willie steeled himself.

'I'm afraid you can't come in, Mr Haliburton.'

Lise began to make a prolonged low sound that was not a groan but an exhalation, like a pair of bellows pressed and crushed flat to expel the last air in a whimper. Willie retreated towards her.

'Willie . . . can you count? You can help me if you can count . . . you have to tell me how many minutes between each contraction.'

'What's that?' he whispered, struggling to recall his Red Cross Handbook.

'It's a sort of pain.'

'Where do you feel the pain?'

'In my back.'

'Oughtn't it to be in the front?'

'If you are in any difficulties,' suggested Haliburton from outside, 'I advise you to report to the First Aid posts, or to fetch someone competent. I believe Dr Florestan, at the European News Desk, has medical qualifications.'

In spite of his predicament, Willie did not really want

Mr Haliburton to go away. Whatever it was that supported the Senior Announcer, his four years at the Western Front, his training under Sir John Reith, his performer's vanity – all these together gave him a superb indifference to the tossing and snoring shambles around him, and an authority which made Willie plead: 'Just a minute, Mr Haliburton.'

Lise groaned again, and this time the noise rose above the permitted level of sounds in the darkened hall. Willie thought he could hear a faint tick, as of liquid splashing onto the floor in small quantities. Meanwhile the Halibut, who had, as he remembered too late, a Deaf Side, passed sedately on.

It's too bad he couldn't rest his leg a bit, Willie thought confusedly.

The prospect of looking after them both – the correct Old Servant and the agonizing girl – side by side under the same too narrow blanket, flashed upon him like a nightmare. Without trying to work things out any further he felt for Lise's damp hand and held it.

'Strike some more matches.'

'I'd better save them, I think.'

'Are you still counting?'

'I can hold my watch to my ear and count the sixty seconds.'

Lise heaved, and now once again she was like a young beast wallowing, and marked out for destruction. While Mr Haliburton had been there, the sleepers nearest to them had remained relatively tranquil, soothed by his familiar voice, reassuring even in a whisper. But now that he was gone they became restive. I must calm her, he told himself.

'I'm not criticizing you, Lise,' he said, bending close to her. 'I believe every human being should follow their own bent, and I assume that's what you've been doing. Probably you didn't envisage this situation.'

She clung on, yet he felt separated from her by many miles. He wouldn't have believed that a girl could grip like

117

that, so that his hand felt numb, with the tarsus and the metatarsus, was that right? – crushed together. The British character was at its finest in adversity. Lise, though, was half-French, if he'd got that straight. In any case, there mustn't be pain like this after the war was over. Everyone, people like himself, must carry a range of simple medication, then you'd be able to be of real help to anyone you happened to meet in a situation like this during the course of the day.

His palm was stuck to hers with sweat like glue.

'Don't leave me,' muttered Lise. 'Go and fetch somebody. Stay here. Don't tell them in First Aid. Go and get somebody straight away.'

What was needed before anything else, in Willie's view, was something to mop up the floor with. He knew every room in the building, as part of a comprehensive survey he'd made of the defence facilities. The nearest cloths and hot water would be three doors to the left, where there was a messenger's room, and they would be off duty now. As he edged out of the concert-hall he saw Mr Haliburton, propped against the wall to ease his leg, and talking quietly to a small group.

'Sir John always expected us to wear dinner jackets to read the late news . . . on the other hand, informality can, I think, be carried too far. . . .'

In the harsh overhead light of the messengers' room Willie felt sick. There was a bath in there, round the inside of which Accommodation had painted a red line, to remind the staff not to use too much hot water. For some reason this red line also made him feel sick. When he looked down and saw that there was blood on his shoes and trousers it became clear to him in an instant that he couldn't carry on any longer on his own responsibility. He had no hestitation at all about where to go for help.

'Mr Haggard, sir.'

DPP looked up from his desk without hope, alarm, or irritation. He could see that the juvenile who had just come

118

into the room was bloodstained here and there, and that as he was not apparently bleeding himself, the blood must have come from somewhere else.

'I don't think you remember me,' said Willie, grasping the back of the visitors' chair.

'I do remember you,' said Jeff.

'You may think it very queer my coming up here to see you like this.'

'Queer, but not very queer. You'd better sit down. I don't think you gave me your name when we last met.'

Willie gave his name. 'Junior Recorded Programme Assistant,' he added.

He felt it would help him not to be sick if he attempted a measure of formality. 'It's Lise, sir, I mean Miss Bernard, really perhaps I mean Mrs Bernard.'

He glanced down at the knees of his grey trousers.

'Perhaps the thought's passing through your mind that I've murdered her.'

Jeff saw that he was in a bad way.

'Never mind what I think. We can discuss that later. Who is Miss Bernard?'

'Well, she's having a baby, Mr Haggard. I suppose she may have had it by now, but these things take some time, you know. That is, she's giving birth to a child, in the concert-hall.'

Jeff paused before replying, but scarcely any longer than usual.

'In the concert-hall, you say?'

'It's one of those curtained off bits, just as you go in. I just happened to be passing. I had a ticket for tonight, that was all in order. No, sir, I'm not telling you the exact truth, I hoped perhaps if it was free I might go in there myself. It's the one next to the door, so usually it's kept for the Senior Announcer.'

'But at the moment it's occupied by Miss Bernard, who is in an advanced stage of labour?'

Willie nodded.

'Is the Senior Announcer in there as well?'

119

Willie shook his head, but with an expression which made DPP ask him whether he was actually going to be sick. Willie thought not yet, and perhaps not at all if he kept his head still.

'Look, William, there are three First Aid Posts on floors one, five, and seven of Broadcasting House, with nurses on permanent duty, and there is also a Home Guard dispensary. I'm only employed here in the capacity of planning the Corporation's programmes. What made you come to me?'

'I thought you didn't really remember me, sir. We were on the Red Cross course together, for all staff without consideration of status. We all thought it good of you to come along, considering you must have seen a lot of casualties already in World War One. In the end we both had the same special chapter for our certificates, sir – frostbite, sunstroke, and sudden childbirth.'

DPP rang through to RPD's office and told him that he had reason to be concerned about two of the junior members of his department. William Sharpe had been made to lie down in the fifth floor First Aid post. Lise Bernard had been sent along the road to the Middlesex Hospital. It was fortunate, since of course there were no ambulances free to fetch her, that his taxi had, once more, been available.

'I don't understand you, Jeff. Have you been knocking them about?'

'Bernard was in the second stage of childbirth, Sam. You remember telling me on a number of occasions that your junior staff, past and present, were a particular responsibility to you.'

'Of course they are. What has that got to do with it?'

'Naturally enough they weren't at all anxious to take her in at the Middlesex, they've got emergency beds two deep in the corridors. We just have to be grateful that hospitals, like the rest of us, enjoy feeling powerful. They allowed themselves to be persuaded.'

'I still don't see why you should have been involved in all this.'

120

'Nor do I. The matron told me some people made the war an excuse for everything.'

Sam appeared to reflect for a while.

'Do you know I'm very glad you told me about this?' he said at last, with warmth. 'I'm very glad indeed that it happened. These two programme assistants, a girl and a boy, who you've never met, who in fact you've never seen or heard of before come to you with their problems, problems, too, of an unfamiliar kind, and although you must have been somewhat bewildered by the part you were called on to play, you did your very best for them – I believe that, Jeff. And that shows that all this appearance of coldness and of not caring a shit for what other people suffer is just what I've always suspected it was, a pretence. I congratulate you, Jeff. You tried to help.'

'That's quite enough,' Jeff replied. 'The time is now 1.47. I'm occupied in sorting out the difficulties of Religious Broadcasting, who want a full-length service of praise and thanksgiving if the unexploded bomb outside St Paul's is removed, but not if it isn't. I rang you because this young woman, as I said, is or was a member of your Department. I think she joined you in May.'

'I wish you wouldn't call my juniors young women, Jeff. They're just girls.'

'Not when they give birth on the premises.'

'I must say I can't see why she should have wanted to do that.'

'You remember the name, I take it.'

'Bernard. Yes, yes, she's been on extended sick leave.'

'Which has now happily drawn to a close.'

'No . . . well . . . she's been away for some time . . . I'm not sure why it was exactly . . . I admit I've rather lost track there . . . you see, Jeff, it's my opinion that the memory has only a certain capacity. The model would be, let's say, a brief-case, where the contents are varied, rather than a sandbag. Under pressure of work, and hindrances, and total misunderstanding, and emotional stress, the less essential things simply have to be thrown out. . . .

121

Something does come back, though . . . I think she was partly French.'

He had forgotten about Willie Sharpe's plight. Lack of curiosity about anyone not actually in the room protected him to an astonishing degree. He might, perhaps, given this protection, last, like some monstrous natural formation, for hundreds of years.

'Sam, are you human?'

'If I'm not, I can't see who is. That reminds me, I don't think I've ever talked to you about a new assistant who's joined my Department, really rather an exceptional person, I don't know that I've ever met anyone exactly like her.'

'Have you got her there now?'

'She's gone to get me a sandwich. By the way Jeff, it's just struck me that all this business, arranging about the hospital and so on, must have been a bit of an inconvenience for you.'

'You mustn't give it a thought.'

11

Lise had always felt that she was particularly unlucky, and furthermore that being unlucky was a sufficient contribution to the world's work. Other people, therefore, had to deal with the consequences. This system worked well, both for herself and her offspring.

There was nothing deliberate, however, in what she had done. After a few nights' and days' drifting, the charitable nuns had taken her in again, as a victim of war's cruel chances, and had arranged for her to go to a good Catholic nursing-home. But on her way back from the cinema she had felt queer, and remembering that she still had her concert-hall ticket she had gone into Broadcasting House for a lie down. The nuns had not liked her going out during the air-raids, or even to the cinema at all, and she was glad not to have to face them again.

Mrs Milne had looked forward to talking over Lise's disaster with Mrs Staples, and had been ready to amalgamate the whole incident, as a narrative, with the bomb stories; morals were relaxed, hearts were broken, while outside the old landmarks fell, and now Harrods Repository had been reduced to dust. But to her amazement Mrs Staples met her braced and poised, as though for a personal attack. When Mrs Milne began by saying that she had no idea where the unfortunate girl was to go to, as her parents seemed unwilling to have anything more to do with her and she could hardly return to the convent, Mrs Staples replied: 'She is coming to me.'

'But what about the infant?'

'They are coming to me.'

'What did they say at the hospital?'

'They were pleased to have somewhere to send her to. I

have a good deal more room on my flat than I need. I think I told you that I found myself talking to the furniture. I shan't have to do that now. Lise is perfectly healthy and I imagine that they'll discharge her soon.'

'You'll never get rid of her!' cried Mrs Milne.

'She didn't stay long at Broadcasting House,' said Mrs Staples calmly. 'However, since I suppose she has received basic training in the work of your Department, I see no reason why she shouldn't eventually return to you as an RPA.'

'And who would look after the child then?'

'I should not mind doing so,' said Mrs Staples. 'He looks quite a little Frenchman already,' she added, and Mrs Milne perceived that she was in the grip of a force stronger than reason.

Willie, without RPD having to be disturbed over the matter, was given a day's sick leave. He went straight to the RAF recruitment centre, but failed to persuade them that he was even as much as seventeen. After that he borrowed an old bicycle from the married sister with whom he lived, and biked furiously up to the heights of Hampstead. It might have been more sensible to get off and push when he got to the last and steepest hill, but such a course did not occur to Willie. By the time he reached the summit, close to the Whitestone Pond, his breath came as painfully as a hacksaw cutting through his ribs. However, he had earned the right to get off and sit on the ground.

He found himself looking for wild plants among the coarse flat grass, just as they'd been made to do on outings from Primary School. Some dusty-looking clover flowers were still out, and two kinds of cudweed, besides the daisies. He collected the hooked pods from a trefoil almost too small to see, took out the tiny black peas, and planted them. Then he lay on his back for a couple of hours in the sunshine. The sky was a limpid blue from one horizon to the other, with no condensation trails, without a cloud, without one aircraft. It seemed to Willie that he was beginning to see things in rather better proportion. Perhaps he might recommend Annie to come up here one day.

Annie, although she had never met Lise, and only knew Mrs Staples from her first interview at BH, was asked round to tea. This was the result of a delusion that Lise needed cheerful company; in fact it made her cheerful to be unhappy.

The RPA rota was improvised from day to day, with unspecified breaks, and Annie had just enough time to get there and back from the address she had been given in Maida Vale. The large flat had certainly been tidy once, but never would be again while Lise was there. Everything seemed to be temporarily out of place, although Lise herself was perfectly motionless on the living-room sofa. The baby, wrapped in a silky white shawl belonging to Mrs Staples, breathed gently, as though simmering, in a wicker basket by her side.

Annie had brought a small pair of socks, knitted while waiting for talks producers. Lise received them indifferently. She let Annie hold the baby, said to weigh eight pounds. Annie could hardly credit that, he felt very warm but light as a doll, staring at her without blinking.

'What'll you call him?'

'I haven't thought.'

'His father was Freddie, wasn't he?'

'Who told you about him?'

'Vi.'

The conversation appeared to be running into silence.

'Do you think you'll return to BH?' Annie asked. She was trying for no more than politeness. Lise, suddenly glowering, burst out: 'That RPD was supposed to look after us all.'

Annie's heart jumped and sprang.

'I can't see what he could have done,' she said. 'From all I've heard, you left without telling anyone.' She added, with an effort. 'Would you like him to come and see you, then?'

125

'What good would that do?'

'I thought you might find it a comfort.'

This wasn't the right word, as she saw at once. She was beginning to sound like the Parish Visitor.

'Comfort!' Lise said. 'He'd only talk about himself.'

'Did you get to know him well, then?'

'He told me I looked like some portrait or other. He was very great on the personal contact. But it wasn't him that took me round to hospital, and he never did remember which portrait it was, either.'

Lise was making an unusual effort. As always, even the thought of Sam Brooks generated energy in unlikely places.

'Someone ought to tell him, Annie.'

'Tell him what?'

'Tell him that he can't deal in human beings the way he does. Mind you, that's what men are like,' she added.

The effort was altogether too much for her, and she began to doze.

Mrs Staples came in with the tea. 'I've brought some of my ration,' Annie said, in the subdued voice appropriate to the subject. Mrs Staples took the little packet and nodded in the same respectful way. Just a cup each, she murmured. The milkman must have been puzzled out of his wits when she'd suddenly begun to order three pints a day, and National Dried as well. Annie reflected that milkmen were hard to surprise, but she didn't say so, for fear of spoiling the drama of the situation.

Annie had to be back at Broadcasting House at 5.30, baby's bottle was due at 6, the bombing, now that the evenings were drawing in, started at about 7, Mrs Staples, who was having a day off, wanted to be in early tomorrow, and for all of them there was the imperative of the nine o'clock news. As long as one was always a little ahead, the battle with the incessant minutes could be called a truce. 'When does he wake?' Annie asked, putting the somnolent baby back in the basket. 'Oh, about ten minutes from now,' said Mrs Staples. He was quietened then with

126

some boiled water from a teaspoon, which he sucked, like an old man with a sweet, contemplatively, and then returned in the form of a fine spray.

Teddy told Annie that it was a known fact that women of every age became broody during a war, and for several years afterwards. There was a straightforward biological explanation of that. Annie was prepared to believe him. But she had only described the baby's activities to conceal her own bewilderment at what was happening to her. She had expected to feel indignant, as always, at any criticism of RPD, she had waited for her indignation to come like the return of hunger or sleep, but when she thought of Lise's remarks, it was missing; without it she was at a loss, and then, worse still, its place was taken by a stranger, a kind of fury, a furious warm urgency to show Lise that she was wrong, but, also, to show RPD that she was right. How was it possible, though, to want to confront a man and tell him that he talked too much, and that he dealt in human beings, and so forth, and still love him? It is possible, her body prompted her. The only trouble is that you're afraid it'll be the end of all things, and then you're ignorant, and don't know how to go about it. But it is possible.

Jeff Haggard resigned himself to being considered the baby's father by most of Broadcasting House. After all, it was generally believed that when the morning mail came in he speeded up business by throwing away every third letter, also that when the French General Pinard had come to the studio DPP had said a few words to him which had caused him to fall down dead. When Barnett asked him, however, whether the Planning Department was to be held accountable for the damage to two blankets and a mattress in Cubicle 1 of the concert-hall, Jeff referred him to Recorded Programmes. The account duly came in, but this annoyance was of the kind from which Mrs Milne protected RPD. She dealt with the matter herself.

127

Precisely at this point, Mac came through on the blower to Jeff to say he had set foot once more in this country to have a look round.

'Still satisfied with your work?' he asked.

If there were any rumours about his resignation, Mac could be trusted to have heard them within a few hours. But Jeff did not reply, because he had no words, even to instruct himself, for the bitter loyalty he owed to the noble, absurd, ungrateful and incorruptible truthtellers whose survival, when peace came, must be precarious indeed. He didn't flatter himself that his withdrawal would be received with anything but relief. Structurally he was a load-bearing element, but one that didn't fit. Everything must look more reassuring when he had been replaced. The BBC, perhaps, counted on his being faithful enough to go. Jeff had a sure feeling for beginnings and endings. It could never be easy to leave, therefore it would be sensible to get into practice. He resolved, as the first break, not to help Sam again with any request, reasonable or unreasonable, or undertake any of the business of Sam's department, private or public, at least for the next ten days. More than that would be unrealistic. But to set a time limit would define his resolution.

This time Jeff came across Mac not in Broadcasting House, but in the darkened street, at the end of Portland Place. The sky was calm that night, with stars and shells high up. At the end of the road the guns in Regent's Park fired intermittently.

Mac was reading the *Evening Standard* by the light of a small fire on the pavement caused by an incendiary bomb. He wore a tin hat and his blue formal suit with a Press arm-band, and had drunk a certain amount of bourbon.

'Who lives in all these places?' he asked, looking at the tall faintly glimmering blocks which curved away like a stage set towards the park.

'One of them's the Chinese Embassy,' said Jeff. 'Sun Yat Sen threw rescue notes out of that window.'

They waited until the whole panorama was lit up by a shower of white magnesium flares, but all the blocks looked much alike. A little later the ground shuddered and they caught the sour smell of bursting gutted rooms as a terrace collapsed two or three streets to their right. 'I'm here to do Britain: the Last Ditch,' Mac observed. 'Every night, twenty forty-five. CBC have booked their circuit at twenty-one hours. Anything they can do, I can have done it better.'

'I've always wondered about your methods of news-gathering, Mac,' said Jeff, accepting a cigar. 'I see you do it in the most economical way possible. I admire you for that. You're preparing to walk straight into LG13, wait for the call-sign, and read them the front page of the *Standard*.'

'You've never appreciated me,' said Mac equably. 'You just want to talk me into making sacrifices. I'll tell you what my network are paying me to do. I'm not broad-casting from the roof of BH because your people won't let me. I'm not doing street interviews because they won't let me do those either. But straight after the lead story I'm giving a summary of opinions from anyone I've talked with in the course of the day.'

'My taxi-driver.'

'You've never let me get near him, chief.'

'He wouldn't help you if you did,' said Jeff. 'He'd prob-ably want your job. He asked me for an audition yester-day.'

Firemen approached to extinguish Mac's small blaze. No longer able to see his paper, he folded it up and put it in his suit pocket. Jeff lit the cigar, which proved in the cordite-heavy air to taste as strong as the canteen's tea. They turned away together.

'Primarily I'm here to find out the reaction of the British people to attack from the air,' Mac continued.

'They don't like it.'

'Then how come they're all hurrying back to London?'

'I don't know,' said Jeff. 'My Listeners' Habits charts

show the population of London as down by a third. That's statistics.'

'Statistics can prove sweet Brer Rabbit,' said Mac. 'I toured the stations this morning and you couldn't move for people arriving with their baggage.'

'Well, after all, it doesn't need explaining. We're only really at home in the middle of total disaster. You'll have to speak up for us, Mac. We're mad, and, if we win this war, we're going to be very poor.'

'Where do we go?' Mac asked. The Devonshire Arms, which he favoured, had been knocked down on the previous night.

'Is there anyone you've got to see?'

'I don't need any personalities, I told you, only the ordinary man.'

'Mac, you don't know any ordinary men. You're a correspondent, you don't have time to meet any. You wouldn't recognize one if you did.'

'I have and I could,' Mac insisted.

'When and where?'

'Want to bet?'

'Five pounds.'

'We're in business.'

Mac thought it best for them both to have a drink on it. 'I'll take you to see an ordinary man now,' he declared, with great intensity.

'What time are you through to New York?' Jeff asked, feeling that he ought to be absolutely sure on this point.

'Twenty forty-five. But I'm not going on the air unless you come with me to see the ordinary man.'

'I'll come with you to see the ordinary man.'

Mac observed that he had made a mistake in looking so often at the flashing sky. Never much good at seeing in the dark, he was considerably worse after tracing the net of searchlight beams and the scattered brightness overhead. However, he'd sent out a stringer the night before to count exactly the number of steps from his flat to Broadcasting House, from Broadcasting House to the Langham, down

130

Regent Street to the Ritz bar. 'We'll head for Trafalgar Square,' he said, and while the night crackled and droned around them he steered Jeff forward, earnestly counting the paces.

They took five hundred and sixteen down Regent Street, where the buses, caught in the raid, waited patiently for a green light. 'I knew a poet once,' said Mac, coming to a halt. The remark had no connection with anything that went before.

'There are poets here too,' Jeff pointed out. 'T.S. Eliot is here. You can see him going to firewatch at his publishers most nights. He moves in measure, like a dancer.'

'He's successful, he's a Harvard man. The one I knew wasn't.'

'In what way?'

'He lost the will go to on. He found he hated to write. Finally he didn't go any farther than the middle of Brooklyn Bridge.'

'These are hard times for poets,' said Jeff. 'Poetry has suffered its fate. Let's only hope that music doesn't follow it.'

'Every man writes poetry once in his life, did you know that?' said Mac. 'Look,' he added, 'we can find some girls later.'

'Keep counting,' replied Jeff.

Down Coventry Street they passed doors with tiny slits of light, just enough to catch the eye. These were the rendezvous for Europe's Free Forces, soldiers who were sad and poor. They turned right and the area of starry sky widened out, showing that they had entered an open space.

'One thousand two hundred and sixteen. Trafalgar Square.'

'I'd say there was a crowd gathering over there,' said Mac. 'Round that truck.' His sight seemed to have improved.

Discreetly shaded lights were moving round a parked lorry, which seemed to be loading up. The men and women concerned moved gravely, pointing their torches

131

towards the ground. If it was a ritual, then it was surely a funeral rather than a celebration. On the lorry was a single huge dark wrapped object, impossible to identify, the centre of all their coming and going. Patiently they were trying to secure the canvas with pieces of string that were several inches too short. Two policemen stood leaning against an empty stone plinth, evidently in two minds whether to help or not.

'What's happening?' said Jeff, speaking to what he could glimpse of an elderly man.

'We have come to move the king.'

He walked slowly off, as if spellbound.

'How come they didn't do this by daylight? asked Mac in amazement. 'When they could see what they were doing?'

'I daresay they've been at it for ages. They're amateurs, and that has its disabilities, advantages too, of course.'

'What amateurs? What have they got on the truck?'

'If this is the south-east corner, it's got to be the Charles the First statue. That makes them some kind of Royalist society. I suppose they're taking him out of harm's way.'

A woman in the darkness confirmed this, saying mournfully: 'The king is going into hiding.'

'Next thing you know you'll have a republic,' said Mac, and then, stepping forward, 'John McVitie, representing the National Broadcasting System of America. Speaking as a sympathetic onlooker, I'd be grateful if you cared to tell me how you set about packaging King Charles.'

'Sawdust,' said another man, this time a very young one. 'But it was a long time coming, so we waited.'

'That's a lot to do for anyone. Can you tell me where you're thinking of taking him?'

Silence, except for London's outer defences, pounding away like a distant ring of drums.

'And naturally you can't say when you expect to bring him back?'

'There will be omens,' said the melancholy woman. The lorry driver was cautiously trying his engine. 'White birds will fly, as they did before the martyrdom.'

'Why not?' said Mac.

Jeff made him sit down beside the boarded-up fountains. 'There's no justice in this thing. Some attract all the love and care. Milton's statue in Cripplegate went on the very first day, but he got no co-operation.'

Mac reminded him that he had said these were hard times for poets. 'I'll tell you something, though, it's upset me that these people should be taking away the king when we're committed to go and see this ordinary man.'

'That's perverse of you, Mac. One thing leads to another.'

Jeff was pretty sure that he'd no idea where to go next; in any case, they only had twenty minutes before studio time. Mac, however, seemed to rally, and they patrolled the square again as far as the mouth of the Underground, marked by a faint glow.

'This is where we go down,' said Mac, counting the steps out of habit, and blinking in the frowsty yellowish light.

On the platform it was difficult to walk freely, since the LPTB's bunks occupied the walls in tiers, and other shelterers had arrived to take their possession of their marked areas, bringing with them folding chairs and tables, and in some cases cooking-stoves. Others were waiting until the live rail was switched off at midnight to spread out their mattresses on the line itself. Meanwhile, the trains were still running, and those waiting to travel in them were confined to the extreme edge of the platform, nervously clinging to their bags and newspapers, aliens, where they had once been the most important people there. The shelterers, though friendly, crowded up to them, nudging them with kettles, and apologizing with the air of those in the right as they set up the evening's games of cards and chess. When a warm block of air preceding a tube's arrival was pushed out of the tunnel, the travellers recovered their dignity for a few moments. The doors opened and they were carried out of reach, while the alighting newcomers got ready to pick their way through

133

occupied territory. Then the night world, created by the violence above ground, settled down, without dispute, to nine hours of their own devices.

At the far end of the platform four men, wearing macintoshes much like everybody else's, were sitting on the ground on a rug. They were playing nap. Each of them had a hand of cards and some of the tricks appeared to have been made, but they sat quietly, waiting. The nearest man, whose face and hair were both between brown and grey, looked up at Mac.

'Glad to see you.'

'How did it come, Mr Brewster, did you win?'

'We're starting the hand where we left off last night. The all clear went at a quarter to five, just after you left. All right, so you're back. What do you advise me to play?'

Mac looked round at the others. 'Any objections?'

They shook their heads amiably. Mac considered, then selected the ten of diamonds and laid it on the platform. Brewster nodded in cautious admiration.

'Just ordinary play,' Mac said.

Jeff wondered whether he had five pounds on him.

When they got back to Broadcasting House Mac went straight to the studio and gave a news talk which was remembered long afterwards, and which in fact was quoted at length in his biography, *According to Mac*. They had counted their steps all the way back, and arrived with twenty seconds to spare.

12

Jeff, who had gone back upstairs to his office, observed the door-handle give an apologetic rattle, or two, then burst open, while the walls curved inwards towards each other with elastic force, and, when it seemed quite impossible, sprang back again. Shortly after this came the sound of water cascading through the intestines of the building.

He was a few minutes late in going down to the basement for the late night Deputy Director General's meeting. To say that he had been for a walk, however, was a sufficient excuse. 'Very hazardous,' ADDG declared. 'It's said there are parachute bombs falling on North London. We've been discussing whether they ought to be called aerial torpedoes on the Nine O'clock. Defence wants that, but the news readers say they can't get the words out. Nobody in the building seems to be able to pronounce "aerial".'

'Ayeerial torpedoes ... airial torpedoes ... ayereeal torpedoes ...' murmured Director (Talks), Director (Public Relations) and Director (Home).

'Who's reading?' asked Jeff.

'It's the Halibut again. We can rely on him.'

'Certainly we can. He started in opera. It takes more than a few bombs to make a singer give up his part.'

The subject of the meeting was the familiar one of how to carry on. Engineering had skilfully ensured that the BBC, switching from one transmitter to another, need never go off the air. Maintenance was probably at work already on the broken pipes, Catering brewed away remorselessly in the basement, but the problem remained: what should the voices say?

ADDG sighed. 'You can't make "Heavy damages and casualties have been reported" sound reassuring.' He wore a kindly, puzzled, clerical frown. 'More encouraging music, I think, and talks from serving airmen, if the RAF will let us. We really look to DPP to shift the next few evenings about, as usual.'

When she felt the building shake Annie went straight along to RPD's office.

'Did I tell you to come?' he asked, slightly lowering the volume of *The Teddy Bears' Picnic*.

'I came to see whether you were all right.'

'Why shouldn't I be?'

'The whole building shook just now.'

'I was testing.' He looked vaguely about him. 'But you can sit down, Annie, I did want to see you, as it happens. I've had something of a disappointment. Let me tell you about it. At certain stages of my work I've been in the habit of consulting a colleague who joined the Corporation at the same time as I did, and might, I suppose, as he's much less specialized, be thought to represent a broader outlook. Now, about half an hour ago, when a totally unnecessary difficulty came up – the Post Office, with ludicrous obstinacy, refused to give me any more land lines – this colleague, who I've regarded hitherto as my oldest friend, wasn't available. He'd gone out with some American or other.'

'Mr Brooks, you can't expect him to sit here night and day just waiting for you.'

The raid was at a low ebb, but there was a curious tension in the air, as though electricity had leaked like water.

'But don't you see, Annie, that some people are born to be deserted? I've tried to put off thinking about it, but this evening it's become quite clear upon me that this kind of failure to help me is part of a pattern, it must be. It can't be chance that it recurs so often. My wife left me, you know ... I don't know whether you, from your short

136

experience, have formed any definite opinion of what I'm like?'

'Yes,' Annie said. 'I've formed a definite opinion of what you're like.'

She saw that he was waiting, and there was no reason why she shouldn't answer him as she had often done before. Certainly there was no call for her to drop all the cautious devices which had enabled her to go through each minute of every day without letting on to him what she felt. Not to give way, not to make a fool of herself, had been such reliable guides that to go forward without them was terrible to her. She felt herself pushed into an un-known country, not, curiously enough, by love, but by anger. Her relief at finding him safe and sound had turned into a kind of rage, which confused her at first, and then left her determined.

'Aren't you going to tell me?' he asked confidently.

'Honest, do you want to know?'

'Honest, I do.'

He was making a joke of it then. She collected her forces.

'You're selfish.'

Still holding *The Teddy Bears' Picnic*, he looked furiously up at her.

'I don't understand you.'

Annie felt giddy, as when a great weight goes sliding.

'There's two ways to be selfish. You can think too much about yourself, or you can think too little about others. You're selfish both ways.'

No-one can calculate the impact of a blow on a man who has never been struck before. Annie lost a little courage as she looked at him, but she went on:

'Take Mrs Milne. She works out her heart on your account. She'd stay longer than half-past five for you if she wasn't a Permanent. Those matches she leaves for you, for instance. There's not many her age would think of a thing like that. But you don't take the trouble to know how she feels.'

After a pause Sam said: 'I do know how Mrs Milne feels. But I don't care.'

His humble tone disconcerted her. He seemed dismayed. Ready to stand up to him without giving an inch, seeing herself given her cards or even thrown out of the office neck and crop, she was caught off balance. He continued mournfully: 'I don't know why it was, Annie, but it never occurred to me that you would be likely to turn against me. I was foolish there, I dare say. We were talking just now about desertions.'

'But I'm not deserting you!' Annie cried. 'It's useful to know yourself!'

'It's painful. That's not the same thing.'

He raised his wounded head. Annie felt beside herself.

'I wish I'd not spoken now. Or at least I needn't have said quite so much. Less is more, sometimes.'

'That doesn't sound like you,' said Sam sharply. 'Who told you that?'

'Mr Waterlow did, when he was explaining to me about Satie.'

'Why are you always listening to music with Waterlow? It's ridiculous. Waterlow is ridiculous. No-one pretends that he isn't, not even he does. It's my belief that you're always hanging about listening to commercials with Eddie Waterlow when you're in fact being employed and paid to do something else. I don't like Satie, either. Hell, I can't stand him. You can listen to music inside your own Department. You can listen to it here in this room if you want to. I played you some Holst once.'

'It was flat, Mr Brooks.'

'I remember your saying that!' Sam roared. 'I nearly fired you on the spot when you said that.'

'There'll be no need to terminate my contract,' said Annie, with a sudden inspiration. 'I'm about to leave anyway.'

'So that's it! Everything you've said so far is leading up to a petty complaint about your hours. I'm well aware that you're all working overtime. As it happens, I'm sending in an application to-morrow for four more juniors.'

138

Now that he was fuming to and fro between his desk and his turntables, as he often did, she felt rather steadier.

'I'm not leaving because of the overtime, Mr Brooks. I'm leaving because I love you.'

Halted on the half turn, he looked almost frightened.

'Do you mean you're in love with me?'

'No, I didn't say that. I said I loved you.'

So deep was his habit of demanding and complaining that he scarcely knew what to do with such a gift. Something had to be done, of course. 'You're very young,' he attempted. 'For some reason Establishment never bothered to tell me anything about when they took you on, but I know you're very young. In a few years' time you'll meet someone your own age – '

'You've read that some time in some book or paper,' Annie interrupted. 'You can't just quite think which one it is at the moment, but it'll come back to you sooner or later.'

He took off his glasses. It was capitulation. He stood reproved now by a delicate blur, the mere shape of a girl.

'I had no idea,' he said.

'That's what I was getting at. You've no idea about others, and you don't notice what makes them suffer. Do you remember the ring with the red currant?'

Sam floundered. 'Did you have one? I think I remember your having one.'

'You gave it me.'

'Have you kept it, then?'

'I would have done, if it hadn't begun to go off.'

She almost felt like asking him to put his glasses back. Otherwise, she wouldn't be able to go on much longer without touching him.

'Dear Annie,' he said to her, 'I don't think I can talk to you here. I want to take you out with me somewhere. There's only one café open now, that's the Demos. We'll go and have a drink and start from the beginning.'

Her happiness was greater than she could bear.

'That'll be very nice.'

139

'It won't be all that nice,' said Sam, feeling compunction, and amazement at himself for feeling it. Annie, for her part, knew that unlike many in BH he wasn't given to feeling he needed a drink. Their lives were shaking into pieces. 'What are we going to do, Annie?' he asked in bewilderment. She put her arms round him. Good-bye, Asra, she thought. God knows what's going to become of you now.

The ADDG's meeting did not last long, and Jeff felt the tenderness of what might perhaps be a last occasion as he ascended to the outer air. On his way up he met Willie Sharpe, carrying a pile of new recordings for War Report.

'Have these,' he said, offering a handful of cigars.

'I don't smoke, Mr Haggard.'

'I didn't think you did. They might come in useful as bribes.'

He was conscious of Willie's round blue gaze, rejecting the word. 'Tell me, do you consider that either myself or your present Head of Department are likely candidates for your new society?'

'Not just as you stand, perhaps,' Willie admitted. 'But a good society transforms its members. By the way, sir, were you expecting to see RPD this evening?'

'Quite the contrary. I don't even know where he is.'

Willie looked faintly troubled.

DPP walked out past Reception, who seized the opportunity to ask him whether he wasn't put in mind of Ypres, passed a word with the sentries, and stood outside, looking up at what he could hardly make out, the carvings of Prospero and Ariel on the stony prow of Broadcasting House. He could very well remember Eric Gill at work on those graven images, high up on the scaffolding, his mediaeval workman's smock disarranged by the breeze, to the scandal of the passers-by. The sculptor and the figures had both appeared shocking then. Now very few people ever bothered to look at them, and that was reassurance in itself.

Prospero was shown preparing to launch his messenger onto the sound waves of the universe. But who, after all, was Ariel? All he ever asked was to be released from his duties. And when this favoured spirit had flown off, to suck where the bee sucks, and Prospero had returned with all his followers to Italy, the island must have reverted to Caliban. It had been his, after all, in the first place. When all was said and done, oughtn't he to preside over the BBC? Ariel, it was true, had produced music, but it was Caliban who listened to it, even in his dreams. And Caliban, who wished Prospero might be stricken with the red plague for teaching him to speak correct English, never told anything but the truth, presumably not knowing how to. Ariel, on the other hand, was a liar, pretending that someone's father was drowned full fathom five, when in point of fact he was safe and well. All this was so that virtue should prevail. The old excuse.

Barnett came out for a breath of air and stood at DPP's side for a minute, looking up not at Broadcasting House, but at the stars.

'You know, I'd give a good deal to be able to read the heavens like a map, Mr Haggard. It'll be my hobby, when we get to the end of all this.'

I don't know why I'm leaving this place, Jeff thought, or these people.

Reception emerged just then, and said that DPP was wanted on the telephone.

'It's an outside call, not a very good line, I'm afraid.'

'Where from?'

'That I'm afraid I can't say, sir.'

'Well, who is it?'

'It sounds like RPD, sir.'

'Jeff, I've been trying to get you. Listen, you know how often I've felt that I needed one human being to rely on, just one, I mean, out of all those millions on millions, someone who'd be prepared to listen when I wanted to talk and perhaps have some kind of understanding, not of

141

my own troubles, but of the troubles other people create for me. You know how often I've said that.'

'Well?' said Jeff.

'And how often, too, I've been disappointed.'

'I know that too. As a matter of curiosity, where are you speaking from?'

'That's what I've rung up to tell you. I want you to come to the Demos Cafe, the Greek place in Margaret Street, D-E-M-O-S, Demos.'

'I'm familiar with the word,' said Jeff. 'I just don't want to go there.'

'Listen. I'm here with one of my RPAs, I think I've told you about her already, I mean Annie Asra. We're very happy. Something rather unusual has turned up, in that she told me not long ago that she was in love with me, no, that she loved me.' Sam rattled the receiver violently. 'Are you following me?'

'I follow you, but I don't quite see how it concerns me,' Jeff said.

'I've told you, I want you to come here at once.'

'No, Sam.'

'Why not?'

'I'm going home.'

'You haven't got a home,' Sam replied, 'Your presence here is essential.'

'Look here,' said Jeff. 'Have you left this girl all this time sitting by herself at a table?'

'She's not by herself. The head waiter is complimenting her on having found a lover. We explained everything. They're all Greeks here, you know.'

'You're intending to live with this girl?'

'I shall take her back with me to Streatham. I've got a house there, you know. With some nice things in it,' he added more doubtfully.

'In that case, there's nothing more that I can contribute,' said Jeff. 'All I can do, like the head waiter, is to offer my congratulations. Kiss her white hand and foot from me, as Petrarch puts it.'

142

'My God, I don't need Petrarch to tell me to do that,' shouted Sam. 'You haven't even begun to get my point. I want you to come here and talk so that you can put my case to DDG in the morning.'

Jeff waited.

'I'm leaving the Corporation, Jeff.'

'Sam.'

'I've handed in my resignation as from to-night.'

'Do you mean that you're seriously contemplating leaving because you're going to sleep with one of your RPAs? Everyone thinks you do anyway.'

'Jeff, you're not trying to understand me. But you have to grant me one thing, whatever else goes I've always prided myself on this one thing, I mean that I've got a proper attitude towards my staff. You were reproaching me only the other day, I can't remember exactly how it arose, but you suggested that I couldn't even remember the name of one of my girls. Well, you see now that you got it wrong. Annie and I want each other, but that un-questionably means that I can't stay in my Department. I can't stay for as much as another week. If I did, what kind of example would that be for my juniors?'

The silence lasted so long that Sam began to rattle again at the telephone. Through the din Jeff could hear the clashing of dishes and even a service lift in the background, also, he thought, protesters anxious to get at the telephone themselves.

'You're my oldest friend!' Sam roared.

'No, I'm not.'

'I want to talk to you!'

'You can't.'

Nevertheless he hesitated.

The BBC never had time to keep any formal archives. There is no adequate account of the deaths of General Pinard, or of Dr Josef Vogel, or of DPP. Everyone who saw DPP that night, however, agreed that his moment of hesitation before he left BH was quite uncharacteristic of him.

The parachute bombs had been coming down soundlessly for some time, and it was later established that one of them was resting, still unexploded, against the kerb in Riding House Street. In size and shape it approximately resembled a taxi, and passers-by in fact mentioned that they had thought it was a taxi. It was understandable therefore that DPP, who appeared anyway to have something on his mind, should walk up to it, and, confusing it in the darkness, try to open what might have been, but was not, a door. Anyone might have done this, but it was tragic that it should have been an Old Servant, and within a few yards of Broadcasting House.

The Assistant Deputy Director General, when doing the obituary, was doubtful, however, as to whether he should describe Jeffrey Haggard as an Old Servant, in spite of all that he had done for the Corporation. Even after so many years, he seemed hardly that. 'His voice in particular,' he finally wrote, 'will be much missed.'

Flamingo

Flamingo is a quality imprint publishing both fiction and non-fiction. Below are some recent titles.

Fiction
- ☐ CHANGES OF ADDRESS Lee Langley £3.95
- ☐ SHILOH & OTHER STORIES Bobbie Ann Mason £3.95
- ☐ BLACKPOOL VANISHES Richard Francis £3.95
- ☐ DREAMS OF SLEEP Josephine Humphreys £3.95
- ☐ THE ACCOMPANIST Nina Berberova £2.95
- ☐ SAD MOVIES Mark Linquist £3.95
- ☐ LITTLE RED ROOSTER Greg Matthews £3.95
- ☐ A PIECE OF MY HEART Richard Ford £3.95
- ☐ HER STORY Dan Jacobson £3.95
- ☐ WAR & PEACE IN MILTON KEYNES James Rogers £3.50
- ☐ PLATO PARK Carol Rumens £3.95
- ☐ GOING AFTER CACCIATO Tim O'Brien £3.95

Non-fiction
- ☐ CHINESE CHARACTERS Sarah Lloyd £3.95
- ☐ PLAYING FOR TIME Jeremy Lewis £3.95
- ☐ BEFORE THE OIL RAN OUT Ian Jack £3.95
- ☐ NATIVE STONES David Craig £3.95
- ☐ A WINTER'S TALE Fraser Harrison £3.50

You can buy Flamingo paperbacks at your local bookshop or newsagent. Or you can order them from Fontana Paperbacks, Cash Sales Department, Box 29, Douglas, Isle of Man. Please send a cheque, postal or money order (not currency) worth the purchase price plus 22p per book (or plus 22p per book if outside the UK).

NAME (Block letters) _____

ADDRESS_____

_____

_____